Me & the '5

A Coming of Age Motorcycle Story

Written by Cyrus Lee

Illustrated by Kevin Poole

Table of Contents

Introduction

When a little boy begins to break away from his mother, he will seek out mentors of both good and possibly bad influence. Some boys make the choices on their own while others get a bit of guidance as they go. If a boy is lucky he gets a good start with his dad; and if that dad is wise enough to expand the network, he can possibly look back with some pride on those he chose or at least allowed in that network.

A slow bloomer, I stayed closer to my mom until a permanent move to Montana, ahead of dad's retirement, brought me into my grandfather's orbit. I had visited my grandpa over the years but now he was around all the time. It seemed that he could fix or build anything for the house or farm. He ran the town grader, keeping the gravel roads free of ruts, and he contracted to haul the bags of mail between the local post office and the mail car at the railroad station.

We moved from Texas as soon as school was over. The folks had bought a fixer upper in town just across the field from Mom's sister. Grandpa was making sure that work was done right so the house would be fit for his daughter; now back in town for good after over 20 years of traveling the world as a Navy wife. He taught me a lot of things about making a living and taking care of family. When you look back on life it seems that kids think things go on forever; the school year, church services, and the lives of adults. Nothing lasts forever.

Dad arrived just after that as fall was waning and winter looming, so the family dug in till spring with school for the kids who were already looking forward to summer. I was planning to start a lawn mowing business. Winter cold waned, spring changed the dead gray browns to brilliant greens. Kid's summer began with the end of school as we downed books for three glorious months...

The individual chapters of "Me & the '53" take you through perspective changes that develop characters in the present tense, then flashbacks to the past to describe how fate intervened to bring Scorchy to town. This takes the Kid on the fast track to being the trusted student-recipient of Scorch's strong code of loyalty and morality, and of his wisdom gained from years of life experiences. The Kid gets an education he could not buy at any cost, anywhere...even an Ivy League family 'pedigree' could not 'learn' that small boy on life the way he learned from a true old 'highway historian'!

The Players

The Place and the Times…

The Kid

The new boy in a small south central Montana town, the Kid learns about life as he is befriended by another new arrival in town, Scorchy Black. The summer becomes one of learning about himself and others as he takes away from "workin" with Scorchy bits of life knowledge. As the summer passes into early fall he learns to look at both those familiar and strange to him in a different way. The Kid enters the summer a child and comes out a boy on his way to being a young man.

Scorchy Black

Scorchy rides into town to take possession of the local blacksmith shop left to him in old Stubby's will. As the story unfolds Scorchy is 27 years old and has left behind his life in Southern California in the motorcycle shop of his friend and mentor, "Ace"

Murphy. Both Scorchy and Ace have become involved in what will become known as the California Biker Wars, and both have left what they have known for years for a new life in Montana. Scorch has been around, as quick with his brain as he is with his fists.

Wanda

Wanda owns a local diner, the third in a line of self-reliant western women. Wanda comes to town from an unknown past, being put off the train after overriding her ticket by 200 miles. In her mid to late 20s she is a survivor looking for something better. From the first day, she sees Scorchy as more than just another guy in town, there are plenty of them.

Rise of the Outlaw Motorcycle Clubs

Within minutes of seeing that the first motorcycle was built in the early 1900s as an economical means of transportation someone keyed on them as a means to go fast, faster than the other guys. Motorcycle sports boomed into the 20s. In California, where bikes rolled year around, flat track courses popped up. Gathering momentum out of the 30s with improvements to the machines, more and more young men rode and formed local clubs for events and comradery.

Following World War II, America was booming and young men were home after risking their lives on a daily basis. For some, back to the quiet was what they sought, while others, who had become adjusted to a life on the edge and pushing the limits, quickly found the replacement for combat on a bike. Clubs sprang up and as fast as the American Motorcycle Association tried to ride herd by sanctioning races, clubs started their own events. Known as "Outlaw Racing Clubs" they would eventually be labeled as the 1% of motorcycle enthusiasts outside of official AMA sanctions.

Like with any organization groups took on different identities and purpose as they grew, then split into new associations, and took on new aspects. Clubs began to grow, as did domination of territory, and in some cases, criminal behavior beyond drunken rowdiness. Into the 60s these clubs began to rise, define themselves and have an impact on those around them. These clubs would become the 1%er, the triple patch holding clubs that made "Hells Angels" a household phrase.

By 1965, more old style racing and riding bikers like Scorchy and Ace were feeling the pressure. Club lines divided more along ethnic lines; Ace, by marriage, falling in on the side of the Mexican clubs and with Ace rolled Scorchy. Like so many Americans before them these two looked to put the past behind, to make a change. They looked to a new frontier, a distant place and saw greener peaceful fields.

South Central Montana

The Clark's Fork of the Yellowstone River winds nearly straight north to Laurel, Montana between the Pryor and Absaroka-Beartooth Mountains from Wyoming. Located in Carbon County, once an intense coal mining area, the fertile valley is home to large and small farms and ranches and dotted with small towns gathered on the rail line. Each town is home to its own culture, history and characters.

The '53

Peter Fonda on his Harley Panhead motorcycle from the movie "The Wild Angels." His bike was the early "chopper" look which had evolved from the more basic "bobbed" style of bike ridden by California clubs and had been made famous in a LIFE magazine photo exposition on the Hells Angels in early 1965. The bike's look and the California license plate was what quickly brought attention to Scorchy when he rode into town.

I met Scorchy in the summer of 1965 when I was 12 years old. I was the new kid in a small town in south central Montana. I was also pretty much a wimp and socially awkward. Try as I might to fit in with the other boys, I lacked two of the most important attributes necessary for success in rural life, the first being that I wasn't — as I was constantly reminded by the locals — "from around here," and second, I wasn't any good at sports. Up till then I had lived a very sheltered life as the son of a naval officer. While that had led to seeing a lot of the world in just a few short years, it hadn't helped me develop much in the way of social skills or athletic prowess. Like Scorchy later said to me, "You've lived around, but you haven't lived."

While my folks were well off, we really had no status. Kid status in that small town was built primarily on what sort of "spread" your dad had or how good of a jock you were. The really popular kids were doubly blessed, but I ended up more or less isolated out on the fringe of small town life. That was a big problem for me, because I had a constant itch to keep busy. Like any preteen boy, I was always dying to find something interesting to do, which led to wandering around town a lot or hanging out down by the Clarks Fork River as it flowed on its way to the Yellowstone. Eventually I found an old, abandoned, ramshackle house — little more than a shack, really — where I fashioned a "hideout" in the attic, and while it provided me with an escape from some of the boredom and a place to call my own, it didn't do much for the loneliness I was feeling. It was shaping up to be one long, boring summer...

And then I met Scorchy.

A typical small town law man's patrol car like Tom might drive. Often purchased used in either black or white, the local sheriff would sometimes hand paint the missing color to create a "black & white." A police two-way radio, spot light and red gum-ball on top finished the conversion.

The way I heard it, Scorchy rolled off the highway and into town with nothing more that the clothes on his back and a few belongings in the saddle bags tossed over the fender of his stripped down 1953 Harley Davidson motorcycle. Tom Bentz, the local sheriff, quickly met up with him as he cruised past the Muller's bar on Main Street. While the likes of Scorchy were welcome to a beer, a burger, and a tank full of the local gasoline...that was about it. The town had a few of its own low-grade hell raisers, but Sherriff Bentz kept them in check with a thumping now and then. Someone who looked like Scorchy, however, was different...a virus somebody sneezed off the highway that needed to be wadded up in a snot-rag and tossed away.

Scorchy had rolled past the IGA grocery store

and flipped a u-turn. He took notice of the sheriff and pulled over to the curb. With a twist of the ignition switch on the dash plate, the big bike stopped it's *"potato-potato-potato"* idling. He pushed out the kickstand and with a long, slow swing of his leg, Scorchy dismounted his ride looking not at the approaching black and white cruiser, but at the storefront. He stretched very deliberately — as if he knew what came next — and slowly turned as Sherriff Bentz eased his cruiser alongside Scorchy's Harley.

As he got out, Bentz noted the black and yellow California tag under the tail-light. Tom Bentz was always cool, never pushy...but folks had to understand that it was *his town.* Scorchy had the look of a cat that knew how it all rolled, but he also played it cool and spoke up right way. Later, Tom would say he was glad he decided to let Scorchy do the talking first.

"Officer," he began, "I'm Scorchy Black."

"Sheriff Bentz," Tom replied. "You lookin' for somebody or something here?"

Neither man moved fast. Neither man crowded the other.

"I am," Scorchy replied as his hand reached towards the front inside of his leather jacket.

Tom's hand drifted slowly to his side. His .45 caliber side.

A .45 pistol like Tom's. The Colt 1911-A1 was carried by thousands of American service men during World War II and Korea. Many made it home and continued use as a working side arm.

Scorchy's hand hovered just over the leather as if in response to Tom's subtle movement. "I'd like to show you something," he said, and then he slowly pulled back his jacket lapel to clearly expose his side and an inner pocket. Tom relaxed a bit as Scorchy unzipped the pocket and pulled out a tattered and dirty envelope. "This is a letter to me from one Bill 'Stubby' Perkins. It contains his last will and testament, witnessed by a local lawyer named John Clark. The will gives me ownership of all Stubby's worldly goods, which if I know Stubby are pretty few and probably well-used."

That brought a faint grin to Tom's face and a little chuckle as well. "You have that pretty much nailed down," he said. "You picked the right place to pull over. That is...well...*was* his shop right behind you." The sheriff pointed at a sign painted on the wall that read simply 'Blacksmith.' "Never was much of a place to look at, but Stubby was a worker and didn't care much about what he or his place looked like. Only left the place now and then. He lived in the back of the shop." He gestured for the envelope. "Mind if I take a look at that?" It wasn't really a question, but not a demand either. The men had come to a place they could move forward.

Scorchy handed it over. "The letter says I can pick up the key to the place at Clark's office," he said. "I'd sure like to see what I have here. I've been riding since dawn and would be happy to get in and hang my coat."

Tom was a rapid judge of character and while he gave the letter a once-over, his people-sense was telling him this was a rough but honest man. A loner, a man not to be messed with, but not one to mess with others either. "Clark is closed for the day," he finally said as he passed the letter back.

Scorchy wasn't a man of constant sorrows, but he'd had his own share of bad news in his life, so this came as no surprise. He knew his face was streaked with road grime, his Levis were dirty, and his leather jacket did not say "sweet and sunny." He was what he had become, but had no chip on his shoulder about what he was. "Can you point me to a place I can park the bike and sleep out tonight?" he asked. "One we can agree on?"

Tom knew everyone in town, better or worse. He knew who was itching to get their hands on Stubby's place and he knew that the farmers needed a smith. "You a smith, Mr. Black?" he asked Scorchy.

"I'm a machinist by trade," Scorchy replied. "Learned metal and welding in the Army and I worked on a lot of heavy machinery and farm equipment in California. I've never worked with horses. Stubby knew my old man and they kept in touch. They were buddies in the Seabees. Stubby was going to leave the place to Dad but Dad told him he was done moving. He and Ma were set on staying in California, so Stubby willed the place to me." Scorchy glanced over his shoulder at the shop. "That's pretty much the story," he said.

Being sheriff amounted to more than just pouring the odd drunk into the jail cell, settling arguments between feuding neighbors, or writing a speeding ticket or two. It meant making quick judgments that might have long-term consequences, good or bad. In that moment, Tom Bentz called it...and decided that Scorchy Black and the town would be good for each other.

"Figure there's no way you could come up with a letter from John Clark," Tom said, "and sure as heck nobody would deliberately come all the way up here from California for anything Stubby might've left 'em, 'cept if they meant to try and make somethin' of it." Tom strolled past Scorchy, towards the empty lot next to Stubby's shop. "I'll show you where Stubby kept the spare key. You can go see John tomorrow."

A sleeve for a 45 RPM Jukebox record featuring the theme from "The Wild Angels." The movie theme shaped the public view of the California bike gang culture while the catchy soundtrack played on the local AM rock & roll stations like KOOK in Billings, Montana.

Word of the new guy ran through town like a chimney fire. Scorchy went from being the new stranger in town to a Hells Angel on the run from the California law by noon the next day. Every kid in town wanted to get a look at him — and especially his chopped motorcycle — but the '53 was now parked inside the shop, way in the back with a blanket tossed over it so most were disappointed.

Cleaned up and wearing an old Navy work shirt and Levis, Scorchy made his appearance the next morning at the local diner, ordering a cup of coffee and some toast. He paid the waitress, Wanda, with change.

Wanda knew broke when she saw it and knew pride when she saw it as well, so she told him that the diner always served four slices of toast not the usual two you get most other places, and that they always put out a jar of jam, a plate of butter, and — if he wanted — a little bowl of peanut butter could be had for the asking. There was coffee till you said stop with all the milk and sugar you wanted.

Scorchy introduced himself as the new town blacksmith and told her he was open for business in about an hour. She said she'd let folks know. On his way out, he asked for directions to the lawyer's office.

"Not hard to find," Wanda said. "Take a right out the door, go up the street to the bank. It's just next door. And by the way, can you fix handles on my trash cans? Mine are all mashed down."

"You bet, ma'am," Scorchy replied. "I'd be happy to fix them for you."

Not dumb, but broke and proud. It was his first job in town.

Mom's folks lived in town and we had visited for years. I never, ever figured we'd ever do more than visit, but as soon as Dad's retirement came up we were Montana bound. It was a shock to me. Him too, as it turned out.

I mowed lawns for spending money. I was in competition with a brother and sister outfit, but my uncle Jim was married to my mom's sister who taught math, so I got all the teachers' lawns. I was quite a sight, pulling my mower down the road with its gas can and a rake and other tools stacked or strapped on. For variety, sometimes I would push the mower instead of pulling it. That old mower was as tough as nails. It had to be as it got more miles being dragged or pushed than mowing! On my way to a job one afternoon, I took a shortcut through the alley bchind Stubby's old place. I'd heard about the Hells Angel who'd blown into town and figured I'd roll on by and sneak a peek.

I first caught sight of Scorchy as he carried all sorts of stuff out of the shop, tossing it into piles and sorting out different types of metal. The air rang with clangs and bangs. I reckon I'd never seen anyone working at something so hard.

I also reckon I was quite a sight, too...standing there in my kid jeans and striped surfer shirt, leaning on my old mower with its gas can and rake tied together with a rope. I wore glasses back then — still do, actually — but in those days parents weren't concerned when it came to how a kid might feel about clothes or glasses. Mine were your classic BCD's — *birth control devices* — as they were sarcastically called later when I was in the Army. It's funny looking back because now they're cool. The whole look was topped off with a flattop haircut. I probably had my mouth hanging open as I gawked.

It might have been seconds or minutes later, but when he said, "Hey, Kid! You mowin' lawns?" I snapped right out of it and stammered out my best Texas, "Yes, sir!"

Scorchy tossed some metal onto its appropriate pile, then turned and walked towards me. He was huge. Weather beaten face, rough hands...I kinda quivered. My mind raced over what my mom might say if she saw me talking to a bona fide "Hells Angel" in the very same back alley I had been told *not* to walk because "you never know what Indians would be sleeping behind Muller's Bar." Just for the record I never saw an Indian go into Muller's, let alone see one come out. They were all down the road a bit as the reservation was east of town.

I was drifting again, but came back about the time Scorchy was saying "...if you break your blade I'll weld it and regrind it for you. What do you say? Won't take you twenty minutes and you can just pile the grass over in that corner."

I think it was when I closed my mouth and didn't answer back with anything intelligible that he figured out I hadn't got it. A lot of adults, myself included later on, would have said something smart, but Scorchy never did that. As long as I knew him, he was never disrespectful towards anyone unless they crossed his line. The second time, I finally got "...I need this lot cut so it looks decent. I've already picked up the scrap metal. I see your mower is fancy and you can adjust how high it cuts. If you don't have wrenches there are some in the shop. When you're done you can pull your blade and I'll grind, balance and sharpen it and..."

I don't know why I said yes.

Probably it was because I didn't think I had a choice. Next thing I knew I was trying to figure out how to do the height adjustment on the mower. You see, I never got to do mechanical stuff with my dad. He hired it done. I did get to do some stuff with Grandpa when we visited, but my mowing career was pretty much "hope and pray" when it came to fixing or maintaining the lawn mower. A little oil now and then, and some gas...the rest was just imitating what I'd seen the Mexicans do to lawns in Texas.

With the hand-crank starter on the top this was considered a real top line lawn mower. Loaded with rake, gas can and other tools of the trade the Kid pushed and pulled a mower like this over the town's cracked sidewalks on his way to his lawn mowing jobs.

Scorchy tossed me a couple of combination wrenches. After ten minutes of knuckle whacking and uttering words I didn't use in the presence of adults, Scorchy came over, flipped the mower on its side, put one wrench on the inside bolt and the other on the outside nut, and uttered the first words of wisdom I would learn from him:

"Righty tighty, lefty loosey."

Like magic, the bolt was loose.

"Stick her in that bottom hole, stick the wheel on her, spin that nut down on her, tighten her up! Righty tighty! There ya go. Got the others?" He walked off, into the shop, without waiting for an answer.

The mower didn't flip for me like it did for him, but I got it up on its side and finished the job. I fired her up and cut his lot, then raked the grass into a pile like he'd asked. I really had no idea how to approach him about working on the blade, but thankfully didn't have to when came out to check my work, said thanks, and told me to pull the blade and bring it inside.

Another daunting task, since I had no idea how to do what he was asking. I knew the blade was underneath the mower so up on its side it went again. I could see a big nut that I hoped was right. I walked over to the shop door where I could hear Scorchy somewhere in the back, and walked in.

A few bare light bulbs illuminated the blackened wood and metal interior of the shop. It smelled of fire, smoke, and burnt oil. Everything was covered with black dust.

"Big screw driver on the bench!" Scorchy hollered. "You'll need at least a one-inch socket...three-quarter inch drive breaker bar's over there in the drawer...red chest!"

He might as well have been speaking in a foreign tongue. I knew screwdrivers, but a socket, I thought, was where you plugged in your electric train or slot car track. I opened the drawer and carefully pulled out the red tool chest, terrified I would drop it on my toe and spill the contents. I secretly thanked my math teacher for teaching me about fractions so I'd know what "three-quarters" meant, and so I was able to recognize it when I saw it etched on the bar. A square peg on the long bar fit into a square hole on the bottom of something that had the same shape on the inside as the wrenches we used before. It said "1-INCH" on it and looked like it could do the job.

I used the screwdriver to scrape off the grass that was plastered all over the underside of the mower. I was borrowing time, hoping for a revelation, because when I put the socket on the bolt the whole thing turned, motor and all! As I scraped like a madman, I didn't hear him walk up behind me. It was probably pretty funny watching me jolt when I heard, "Hey, Kid, you know how a motor works? To start it you pull that rope on top. That rope turns that same shaft you are turning now. When you turn it fast enough the motor starts unless it can't get spark or gas or air. So let's be on the safe side and pull the plug wire." He didn't wait for me to do it he just did it. "Ah, okay, you cleaned out the hole where you can jam the blade."

I looked and saw a hole. My brain was racing as I put the screwdriver in the hole and turned the breaker bar. The blade jammed on the screwdriver and I could put both hands on the bar and push. It was tight. I tried again. "Righty tighty, lefty loosey," I muttered over and over again. Not a budge.

"Oh, Kid, you know about reverse threads?" Scorchy said. "They make those so stuff won't come off when they're running. Should have told you. Just reverse it."

So I tried a righty loosey. There was a creak and a crack...and off the nut came!

There are few feelings like figuring out something and doing it. When I turned to see what Scorchy had to say he was gone. Being a neatnick, I picked up the nut and washers and put them in my pocket and then went back into the shop.

While I wanted praise, all I got was, "Ok, Kid, you got it."

I let my eyes drift around the shop as they grew accustomed to the light, then I spied the leather jacket on top of a blanket in the back of the shop — a BIKER jacket!

"Hey, Kid, this is gonna take some time," Scorchy said as he eyed my mower blade. "You really got a lot 'a things to fix but a deal is a deal. I'm gonna to have do some brazing, grind it and then heat and temper it. I was supposed to go over and get one of the trashcans from behind the diner. I told Wanda I'd fix the handles. Think you can go get it?"

Again what was I going to say? He had my mower blade, my mower was taken apart, I was late for the job, but Mr. Jon wasn't at home anyway. I'm sure my mom would have a fit if she knew where I was. I heard the words come out of my mouth, "Yes, sir. I can do that." I knew the diner. Mom and Grandma called it a greasy spoon. We never went there, but back in Texas I had gone to a greasy spoon restaurant when I spent the summer on a ranch with my friend David. David was the son of my 4th grade teacher. She and my mom had decided that it'd be good for us to pal around all summer on their ranch. Those adventures are a story for another day, but on Friday nights when the work was done, David's dad would pack us all into the truck and head for town to a place they called "The Greasy Spoon" to eat great hamburgers!

Out in the alley these metal trash cans took quite a beating. The ones behind the dinner were in even worse shape.

When I arrived at the diner, I walked through the door and spotted Wanda's red pony-tail behind the lunch counter. She'd been running the local cafe since we'd got to town. The boys talked about Wanda, as did the women. I got her attention and said, "The blacksmith sent me for one of the trash cans."

"Oh? You working for Scorchy?" Wanda asked.

Wow! Me working for a Hells Angel! A strange feeling rushed through my body as I put my best "Yes ma'am" out there.

"Well, come on back through the kitchen," Wanda said. "Take the empty one and then come back right away."

I thought about dragging the garbage can back through the kitchen, but something stirred in my brain that had the good sense to know that wouldn't be smart, so instead I went back down the alley. I should point out these were not the run of the mill rubber cans everyone uses these days. Wanda had honest to god galvanized steel trashcans. The handles were smashed flat, so my journey was one of grunting, dragging, and roll-ing until I got it to where I had to cross the street. I had to get the can over the ditch next to the sidewalk, across the street, down the other sidewalk to the lot next to Stubby's shop, and then down to the rear door.

When I broke cover at the end of the alley, I spotted a few of my "school chums." I stopped and dropped the can. How could I carry this monster with any sort of pride? I suddenly thought about how I'd used a screwdriver to jam the mower blade, to do more than screw screws. I looked around for a second and a wad of old bailing twine laying in the alley dirt caught my eye. I grabbed it and started feeding a strand between the can and smashed handle. Soon I had a temporary rope handle. Grabbing on I crouched and worked my way under the can and stood up.

Two things became clear upon the initial hoist: one, it was heavy and awkward; and two, it wasn't called a trash can for nothing. The insides reeked from being set out in the sun and the outsides were splashed with kitchen grease. I had to go for it while I had a good grip. Across the street, up to the lot, and then down to the shop back door...halfway across the street my hand was practically shouted at me because the twine was sharp and cutting into me. As I finally hit the opposite sidewalk, one of the kids — Sly — finally spotted me.

"Hey! Cal!" I heard him cry out, "You stealin' trash cans? Yuck, yuck, yuck!"

I have never been happy with my ability to come up with quick and clever comebacks. I've gotten better over the years, but as a kid I plain sucked at it, just like I sucked at just about everything. Without saying anything back, I just kept going, but now my arm had joined the pain chorus and my brain was telling me that every germ and bit of garbage slime in the universe was sliding down my back. The sun's heat had brought out the can's natural aroma and I was staggering a bit as I tried to keep just putting one foot in front of the other. I finally lurched into the lot next to the shop and headed for the back door.

"Come on," I heard Sly say. "Let's see what he's doing." I could hear them coming up behind me. I turned the corner towards shop, and there was Scorchy.

"Hey, Kid," he said. "Looks like you got a load."

He was helping me set it down when Sly and the other boys rounded the corner. Since Stubby's death the lot had become a cut-through to the alley and the town beyond. Habit brought them head long into Scorchy and me.

"Ok, Kid," Scorchy was saying, "Did she say when you could pick up the other? I got the blade done so you can get it back on that mower and then it's going to be lunch time."

I was sweaty, somewhat garbage encrusted, and my hand and arm hurt like crazy. Behind me, I could swear I heard jaws hitting the ground, and then one of those whispers kids make that they don't think anyone can hear: *It's the Hells Angel!*

"Wanda says I need to come right back," I replied. "She has something she wants to give me." I wished I could've thought of something cool and clever to say, but it was enough to let Sly and his buddies know I was "working" for Scorchy.

"Ok, Kid, don't keep her waiting."

Then I was off, right past the boys, high-tailing it for the diner. When I got there, I hit the door hard, which brought up some heads, but, well...kids will be kids when it comes to slamming doors.

Wanda was freshening up a trucker's coffee. She flashed him a smile. His gaze followed her walk over to me. When she bent over the lunch counter it was impossible not to notice that her white waitress dress fit snug on her body.

"Here you go," Wanda said, handing a paper sack to me. "Tell Scorchy I can pay in meals. There's something in there for you, too."

"Thanks, ma'am!"

Heads were turning and gawking. A couple, I knew, knew my dad.

"It's Wanda, honey."

"Thanks.... *Wanda.*"

I headed out the door and I swear I felt taller as I made my way back across the street towards the shop. I could see that Sly and his gang were heading down the street as I walked through the back door.

"Hey, Kid, what you have there?" Scorchy asked, eying the sack in my hand.

I repeated the message as I handed it over. "Wanda says she can pay in meals."

Scorchy reached into it and started pulling sandwiches out of the bag. "Looks like plenty for two," he said. "You want to eat before you put the blade back on the mower?"

I didn't have to say Wanda had told me there was some for me, Scorchy just offered. Maybe he knew, maybe he would have offered half of one sandwich. Maybe Wanda told him later, maybe she didn't.

Sandwiches never tasted better, even with water from the rusty tap on the shop sink. When I finished, I walked over to the edge of the forge where my mower blade hung. It looked like new, the honed edges glowing and razor sharp. Scorchy didn't say anything about being careful, but I was, nonetheless, when I took it down.

I carried it out and "lefty, tighty-ed" her back on. As I carried the tools back in and put them back in the chest and put the chest back in the drawer, I felt different. I didn't have any fear of dropping them at all.

"Hey, Kid."

I turned to face Scorchy. He stuck out a huge hand. "I'm Scorchy Black."

I shook his hand. "I'm Cal Lee."

"Thanks for the help with that trash can, you better get on to your other job. Stop by anytime."

The Shop's First Break

A local farmer topping the beet crop prior to harvest. The tops are piled into rows to be collected and used as food for cattle. This machine used the blades that the Kid helped Scorchy sharpen.

The summer of '65 gathered momentum after my first meeting with the town's newest attraction, Scorchy Black. After his arrival, Scorchy began an earnest campaign to make a living by...well...by the way he lived his life in the new town.

Right off the bat, Scorchy had to keep consumption of his main food source to a minimum as Wanda only had two trashcans that needed handles fixed. Wanda was generous, but Scorchy had been around long enough to know a thing or two...that "fair is fair," any man who just works for food never buys new welding rod, and that there is an acceptable limit to what a man takes from a woman — no matter how well meant — before there are social consequences.

For my part, I understood some of what Scorchy meant; but being pretty dependent on a woman, my mom, for my needs, I chalked it up to being an "adult" thing. I loved the "fair is fair" thing and started using that in just about every other sentence I spoke. At first it was because I felt it might show the adults I was speaking to that I was somehow endued with an adult-ism that was not profane, and then finally it became habit.

You could see most of town from any street that branched off the two-lane highway heading towards Wyoming, so learning his way around town was not hard during Scorchy's evening walks. Dressed in Levis, a denim work shirt, and engineer boots, Scorchy never spared the "good evenings" or shied away from an outstretched hand. His intro was always the same, "Good evening, sir, I'm Scorchy Black. I'm the new blacksmith in town." He never asked for work. He always let the other person bring up some possible project during the ensuing conversation, and there was always a conversation because everyone wanted to know about the new man in town.

When folks engaged him in conversation, Scorchy chatted a bit, but mostly listened. Often it was about the young men who'd enlisting in the military after they had graduated. The red dragon was stirring South East Asia in a place called Vietnam and the President was escalating our support of allies there. Many local boys figured to get in before the draft. Scorchy sometimes mentioned he'd served in the Army in Germany and that military life could be interesting. It turned out Scorchy's time in the Army *had* been pretty interesting, to be sure, but that's another chapter.

Scorchy didn't belabor his conversations. He would finish with, "I'd be happy to take a look at that (iron work-welding-shoeing) you need done. When would be a good time to come by?" If a time and place didn't materialize, he'd eventually excuse himself and head back on into his stroll. Scorchy carried a small notebook and pencil in his shirt pocket and would carefully write down the potential customers' names, addresses, phone numbers (if they had one), and their "project." He told me one time that when he had walked on a bit he'd stop and jot a note about the person's looks to help him put them in his mind since knowing folks was important to getting well known. I picked up the skill of note taking, but never have I master the art of putting names with faces like Scorchy did.

A few lawn mower blades, a tool or two that needed spot welds, a bit here and a bit there...Scorchy lived lean. He was used to having it slim and pocket change always got coffee and toast at the diner each morning. The coffee cup never ended, and neither did the milk and sugar that came with. The toast still always had four slices with all the peanut butter, jelly and butter a customer could want. Scorchy had noticed that other customers didn't want four slices, but he wasn't about to start "spittin' into the wind" at Wanda's generosity.

"Spittin' into the wind" was another Scorchy-ism I picked up right away. Again, I figured this was a mysterious adult-ism meaning something along the line of not doing something. Only a bit later, one windy day, did I figure out that it was more than that. It meant don't do something that will come back at ya! I also learned that "pissin' into the wind" worked the same way.

Sugar beets and beef were the main staples of the farmer-ranchers of the area, and when the beets poked their leaves though the ground, it became time for local kids and migrant workers to start thinning and weeding the fields. A sharp hoe was the critical tool for this job. Scorchy quickly figured out the best way pull the iron end, clean it, heat it in the forge to pound out dents and bends from the previous year's abuses. He'd then dunk the head in tempering oil with a crackling sizzle and, before the oil smoke cleared, put grind a razor-sharp edge on it. He always made sure the handle sleeve fit snug, then he'd take the handle and give it a quick swipe with a wet rag dipped in a bit of sand followed with a wipe of linseed oil before reattaching it. I'll never forget the first time I saw him reattach the handle.

For me it was an education in physics and language. He took the head in his left hand and the handle in his right while I watched intently.

"Hey, Kid, watch how this goes," Scorchy said. "First you put the male end into the female end..."

My jaw dropped. I was twelve and not completely unaware of the "birds and the bees," though in those days the public school system had not yet taken on sex education as part of its curriculum. The only discussion of the topic went on in the locker banter between a bunch of kids who knew little more than what they had heard from older boys. This was rural Montana and you were supposed to be learning while watching the cattle, horses, sheep, dogs, and other living things around you do their business. I don't think many of us got the whole picture, but the point is, I had never heard an adult speak plainly about such things. Scorchy grinned and said something about how I should probably talk to my dad about that. I can tell you that conversation never happened and I think Dad would've rather chopped off his hand than talk to me about sex. But to be fair I, think I wanted it that way as well.

"OK, Kid, you push the handle into the sleeve," Scorchy said, still grinning. What happened next was a mind bender. Scorchy took the hoe handle and tipped the head down towards the floor and reached for the hammer on the anvil. With just a couple of inches exposed above his fist, he smacked the end of the handle a couple of times. I was sure the head of the hoe would drop on the floor, but instead it moved *backwards,* and tighter on the handle. Setting the hammer back down on the anvil, he ran his hand up and down the handle and gave the whole thing a shake. He did this with one hoe after another. Some needed to be smacked a few times more than others before being set in neat rows. When he was done, they all looked like new.

"Hey, Kid!"

I got used to being "Kid" to Scorchy. In fact, I kind of took it as a mark of pride, and if he had called me most anything I would have been good with it. I was "workin" for Scorchy, the "Hells Angel" and that was plenty cool for a kid just out of the sixth grade.

"Hey, Kid...You know where there's some clean sand?"

"There's a sand bar down at the river bend, you want me to go get some?"

"Kid...Grab that bucket by the door, if you wouldn't mind."

And I was off like a shot because it was another "job" I was working on for Scorchy! I had gone as far as the railroad tracks when I realized the river was over a mile away. The bucket was a heavy duty, galvanized two-gallon and already seemed to be gaining weight. Nevertheless, I put my head down and trotted on.

I soon passed my hideout and climbed under a fence and down to the river. The sandbar yielded some fine, clean grit. I scooped the sand with my hands till the bucket was full. Leaping up, I grabbed the handle...and my body stopped in mid extension while the bucket remained firmly grounded on the sandbar. With both hands I strained to lift it. Succeeding (barely), I waddled several steps. The bucket banged both shins and I set it down. The prospect of a mile-plus journey back to the shop loomed black on the horizon. The prospect of disappointing Scorchy loomed even blacker.

The "lift and waddle" was replaced by the "bend over drag" in short order. I could still hear the river. A few scoops of sand fell to the ground. More lift and waddle followed by more bend over and drag. More sand falling to the ground. Repeat, repeat, repeat, repeat until I could stand up and walk. The afternoon had waned by the time I finally darkened the shop door again.

"Hey, Kid! There ya are! Bring that sand on over."

My kid heart wanted to hear Scorchy mention how much sand I had lugged and if all had gone well. My new, little bit more grown up heart was learning that wasn't how it worked at work. "Nice, clean lookin' sand," he said, which was more than I expected.

"Got it at the river," I replied, reveling in the praise as the sun finally shone through!

"OK, Kid, let's get to work. Get a little of that sand on the wet cloth and rub down those hoe handles then set 'em outside in the sun to dry."

I learned that a little water on the rag, plus sand (not too much as I valued every grain) with a bit of elbow grease applied in even long pulls, cleaned up the wood. The used sand hit the floor and a separate bucket held clean water into which the rag went after every swipe so nothing dirty contaminated the clean wood. A second clean rag wiped the handle and out in the sun they went. When dry, a third rag (a piece of an old wool shirt) applied the linseed oil.

"Easy does it, Kid," Scorchy told me. "Only so much'll go in and any hittin' the floor is wasted."

I got it down. I didn't waste any, and to this day I hear that voice as I put a little bit of this or that on a rag to clean something. I'd never been poor, though my folks had both grown up during the depression. That's what took Dad out of Montana and into the Navy...well that and the war. Mom's folks lived in town and Grandpa never wasted a board or nail. Grandma never wasted an egg she could cook or a cloth scrap that could become a quilt. In our house there was plenty.

Dad saw to that, and Mom made sure it was all there for my sisters and me. But with Scorchy there was "enough" and that was "good to go." As beet season came on, preparations for harvest time went into gear. To harvest the beets, all the farmers used a topper with sword-like blades that rotated low to the ground to cut the green leafy stalk off the top of each plant. The folks at the sugar beet factory didn't want that part, not that the farmers wanted to give the stalks away anyhow as they could be used for cattle feed. The blades had to be razor sharp to do their job, but because they worked near the ground they would get dented, dulled and, and broken by rocks buried in the soil. One Monday morning it seemed that someone from every farm in the valley was waiting at Scorchy's shop when he came out of the diner, all eager to get their blades sharpened. I walked through the back door about five minutes after the opening bell.

"Hey, Kid!" Scorchy called out as he hustled. "I need ya to hustle over to the grocery and see if they got shoe tags. Here's a buck. If they're more, tell 'em you'll bring it at lunch!"

I knew the grocery wasn't the place to find the shoe tags. Instead, I went over to the drug store that wasn't really "drug" store anymore, but had become a five and dime soda dive where the older kids hung out and listened to the juke box. Mr. Rilley — people usually called him "Old Man Rilley," "Smiley Rilley," or just plain "Smiley" — ran the joint. Early morning noise was frowned upon as it was common knowledge that Smiley spent his evenings drinking at Muller's Bar. I didn't want any problems so I held back at the door, holding my hand over the bell to keep it from dinging. Red-eyed, Smiley looked up from his morning paper. All he could muster was a look that said, "What do *you* want?"

"Shoe tags?"

Rilley pointed to the back shelf where I found a box that read. "Tag, Shoe, Manila Stock with String, 50 each — $.50." I did the mental math. I'd seen at least fifteen guys in the shop and they all had at least 4 blades. "Got another box?" I asked. I must have been too loud, because Smiley grimaced as he got off the stool and parted ways with his coffee to head toward the back. He came back a few minutes later. I was drumming my fingers nervously on the counter top.

"You gotta make all that racket?" he grumbled.

I stopped abruptly, my fingers suspended in air for a moment, but for some reason I resumed the cadence, catching a beat just my fingertips caught wood. I looked around. There was a lot to see in the shop. There were posters of Elvis and other rock stars above the juke box, the latest tune by Sonny & Cher popped into my head... *"and the beat goes on...the drums poundin' a rhythm in my brain...ladedadede... ladedadedi..."*

45 record of Sonny & Cher's hit "The Beat Goes On."

"Damn it, kid...I told you to shut it!"

I was rocked back on my heels. I could do the kid grovel, but I was "workin" and I didn't feel like groveling. In the back of my head, I worked out a response.

"Two boxes for a buck."

I slapped the George Washington on the counter, a little loud. "Good tune," I said. "Heard it on your Rock-o-la!" I grabbed the second box ad turned away. Exit style was critical. I crossed the floor and made sure the door swung wide to ensure I got a good ring out of that door bell, and a nice crack when door met jamb. Not a bad bang, I thought, as I jumped the sidewalk ditch.

"Got 'em, Kid?!"

Scorchy pulled a pencil from behind his ear and with one fluid motion it was on its way to me. It was in the air, slowly rolling end over end, with all the makings of a total disaster if I was to miss the catch. I missed everything thrown to me, from coins to baseballs and footballs. I was backing up, one hand holding the boxes of tags, the other slowly coming up to catch the pencil. Time crawled and the prospect of embarrassment grew. It was inches from me now and I know I was going to choke. It seemed that every eye was on me.

One of the guys who was in line just snatched the pencil out of the air like an eagle. He handed it to me without expression. No smirk. No smile. I opened the first box of tags and stuffed some in my pocket before putting pencil to card stock.

"Charlie Spennser, right?"

He nodded.

"How many?" The first became last as the end of the line became the front as I wrote his cards and tied them in the bolt holes of his blades.

Scorchy moved over to a flat iron table. "Just set 'em here, we'll have 'em tomorrow."

Using my best printing, I worked my way up the line. I made sure I got the initials of the Baurer brothers as I wouldn't want to mix up *their* blades. All these guys were old school and probably knew the maker marks on their blades. Like some men bought only Ford, they only bought International Harvester.

By the time I was to my third customer, Scorchy had the bellows fan on high and the forge had started to heat up. By my fifth customer, it was glowing and he had Spennser's first blade heating.

Using a big pair of tongs, Scorchy pulled the white-hot blade out of the forge and set it on the anvil. Scorchy started to work with his hammer, taking out bumps and smoothing flat the heated steel. He'd hit it for a while and then turn the blade on edge and eyeball it. If satisfied, it went into a beat up 55-gallon drum of black oil, snapping and sizzling and giving off an aroma of heat and work.

"Hey, Kid!" Scorchy said. "Get that leather jacket off the bike and put it on! Get that hard hat off the post, the one with the face shield, and put on some gloves and come on over!"

I knew of the legendary bike under the blanket. I had caught glimpses of it now and then, but now I was going to actually *touch* it! Well, at least I was going to touch the blanket. I was also going to put on Scorchy's motorcycle jacket!

Scorchy's leather jacket. Harley Davidson wings on the back with a small Ace Murphy's Motorcycle shop wing on the front. Scorchy tells Kid to wear the jacket as protective gear when they are working near the oil bath. Scorchy Black Collection.

I went over to the bike and picked up the jacket. Right off I could feel the miles in the leather, the adventure, the freedom in the wind. At least in my mind I could. The leather was either brown going black or black going brown, I couldn't tell; but I saw right away as I looked at the back there was no "Hells Angels" patch. There *was* a big set of gold wings, embroidered with metallic thread that had an orange shield with the Harley Davidson logo sewn on the bottom. On the front there was a pair of smaller silver wings with a green shield that said "Ace Murphy's Motorcycles, Est. 1940." Nobody with any reliability had said Scorchy was an Angel. That rumor just sprung up spontaneously the day after he hit town. But then, who knew but me...

"Hey, Kid! Get that stuff on an' over here," Scorchy said, breaking my train of thought. "You can look at the bike when we are done!"

The time from the forge, to the anvil, and finally to the oil is critical in tempering the steel. My job was to, "Keep the flow, man!" by moving the blades to the edge of the table, removing the tags and placing them in order. When a blade in the oil stopped sizzling, I pulled it out, let the oil run back in the 55 gallon drum, and then put it back on the end of the table, replacing the tag. The heating, truing, and quenching process was not too speedy for me to keep up. I'm actually pretty sure Scorchy could have done it by himself and maybe we saved a half hour by the time they were done, having worked into the afternoon.

"Ya know, Kid, this is gonna help me make it in this town." Scorchy looked at the long row of blades on the table, all now looking like new. "These farmers want to know they can count on you when they need a job done. We just showed we can do what we say we can do."

I suddenly felt that rush of preteen chemicals pulse through my body. Scorchy had said *"we!"* I pulled the helmet off my head and put it back on its nail. I set the gloves back on the bench, but left the jacket on.

Scorchy fished around in his pocket pulling out some change. "Kid, here's a couple of nickels. You fly an' I'll buy, grab us a couple of cold Cokes." I turned to head out the door.

"Leave the jacket in the shop."

I suppressed the whine that sometimes helped me get my way with my parents. It wasn't going to fly with Scorchy. I shrugged out of the jacket and was surprised at how the weight lifted off my shoulders. It was a lot of leather. I laid it on the rack by the door and then headed for the grocery store where they had the pop cooler with bottles on ice.

I made a studied effort to not drink my Coke in big kid swills. Scorchy sipped his. He rolled the sweet syrup over his tongue, pausing for what seemed hours between drinks. He'd tell me later that's how you "stretch a break." Just like always knowing where a broom is, I'd put that to work later in life.

Five o'clock was edging up on us. I'd be heading home soon, and as always Scorchy didn't forget a promise. "Let's go see how that bike is. I haven't even had a look at the oil since I rolled in." Scorchy gently pulled the old army blanket off.

The shop was always dim, lit only with a couple of bulbs hanging from the ceiling, and my eyes had to adjust to the light. Orange-yellow flames, that's what got my attention first. Flames and Scorchy. A quick connection formed as I took in the paint job on the tank. The flame tips reached back to a black leather seat for one. Two chrome exhaust pipes with ends that looked like shark tails swooped up to the top of the flat rear fender. My eyes, probably stupid wide by now, worked back to the front of the bike. Mounted low in the center of the frame was the V-twin Harley Davidson motor, sparkling here and there with chrome. More chrome accented the handlebars and single headlight. Black forks straddled a chrome front wheel and narrow tire. This was the "west coast chopper" look. A year later, Peter Fonda would make it known coast to coast and then around the world as he and Nancy Sinatra rode across the movie screen in "Wild Angels."

The sound of Scorchy's voice pulled me back into reality. "She's a '53 pan," He said. "I built her when I worked for Ace Murphy..." His eyes focused on the bike, for a moment Scorchy seemed to go someplace else himself. "...a while back. Needs to be started. Wanna give it a try?"

I couldn't believe my ears.

"Climb on," he said.

And with that I passed through that portal, into a new world.

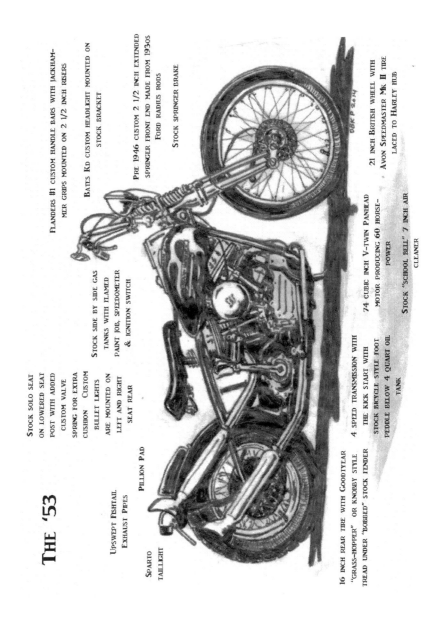

THE '53

FLANDERS #1 CUSTOM HANDLE BARS WITH JACKHAMMER GRIPS MOUNTED ON 2 1/2 INCH RISERS

BATES KD CUSTOM HEADLIGHT MOUNTED ON STOCK BRACKET

PRE 1946 CUSTOM 2 1/2 INCH EXTENDED SPRINGER FRONT END MADE FROM 1930S FORD RADIUS RODS

STOCK SPRINGER BRAKE

STOCK SOLO SEAT ON LOWERED SEAT POST WITH ADDED CUSTOM VALVE SPRING FOR EXTRA CUSHION CUSTOM BULLET LIGHTS ARE MOUNTED ON LEFT AND RIGHT SEAT REAR

STOCK SIDE BY SIDE GAS TANKS WITH FLAMED PAINT JOB, SPEEDOMETER & IGNITION SWITCH

21 INCH BRITISH WHEEL WITH AVON SPEEDMASTER MK II TIRE LACED TO HARLEY HUB

74 CUBIC INCH V-TWIN PANHEAD MOTOR PRODUCING 60 HORSEPOWER

STOCK "SCHOOL BELL" 7 INCH AIR CLEANER

PILLION PAD

UPSWEPT FISHTAIL EXHAUST PIPES

SPARTO TAILLIGHT

16 INCH REAR TIRE WITH GOODYEAR "GRASS-HOPPER" OR KNOBBY STYLE TREAD UNDER "BOBBED" STOCK FENDER

4 SPEED TRANSMISSION WITH THE KICK START WITH STOCK BICYCLE STYLE FOOT PEDDLE BELOW 4 QUART OIL TANK

First to Fight

One of the Flying Tiger P-40 aircraft in Kunming, China. For Ace and his crew, maintenance seemed to only stop when the planes were flying against the invading Japanese bombers.

My sister, Holly, was always getting the dolls Mom brought back from China in 1948 out of Mom's cedar chest. A small brass lock with a key shaped like a Chinese character fit into a matching opening in a lock that kept the chest — Mom's treasures safe — secure. The locking mechanism looked like a set of thin brass bars soldered to the end cap. When you pushed in the key, the whole lock came apart and the chest could then be opened.

By the summer of 1965, China had changed. After the Communist Reds had taken over the mainland, the Nationalists lived in exile on Formosa or Taiwan. The defeated Japanese, of course, were still a resented enemy. But before all that (just a few years after VJ-Day), Dad and Mom had actually lived in Shanghai. Dad was a US Navy pilot and he and my godfather had run the air transport for the Navy there. It was a time of society, parties — and I'm sure some intrigue — as well as a time for buying of furniture and antiques like the cedar chest with the intricate brass lock.

When a piece of the lock fell off while my sister was opening the chest, she brought it to me.

"Take it to work and fix it today," she said hopefully. "Then it will be okay, right?"

There was a strange value in being asked to do something "at work" and in my lil' sis believing I could actually fix it. I could see where it had come apart and I was sure it was metal Scorchy could fix.

"No sweat, Sis," I said, and into my pocket it went.

Midsummer 1965 in Montana. Cool nights gave way to warm, then hot, days. After a breakfast of a new cold cereal that had freeze-dried fruit mixed in with corn flakes, both of which got soft in milk, I walked up River Road towards town.

The railroad crossing arm was down with its lights flashing and bell clanging. An eastbound freight train was rolling through. Nearly every open boxcar had a couple of guys — bums or hobos, Mom called 'em — standing or sitting in the doorway. Most were friendly enough to wave back at a kid who waved at them.

Once I told Scorchy I saw some bums ridin' on the freight train. He said some guys riding the rails were bums, but bums weren't just on trains. Some lived in town. My mind pondered that. I had heard Mom talk about hobo camps that she had seen as a girl in Bozeman. I thought that was what Scorch meant, but I sure didn't know where the camp could be and that would be something a kid would know. Later I learned that he meant being a bum meant something more than just being low on dough or down on your luck.

The shop door was open and I walked in to hear the low roar of the forge. Something needed fixin' and maybe he'd put the lock in the forge. I walked past the covered '53 and then stood quietly while Scorchy pulled a piece of near white, glowing steel out and began to shape it on the anvil. No interruptions. Every second counted as he worked the metal into its final form. Scorchy held it at tong's length, rotating it this way and that, before he then put it into the cooling barrel. When the steam and hiss diminished, I felt it was safe to announce my arrival.

"Hi Scorchy!"

"Hey, Kid!" came back at me, Scorchy didn't turn until he'd laid the work on the metal table top. "What 'cha know?"

I fished the lock out of my jeans pocket and held it out. "I know my sis is goin' to owe me cause she broke this lock and I told her I'd...we'd...ahhh...you could fix it."

Scorch pulled off a leather gauntlet and held out his hand. "Let's take a look at that," He said.

As I put the two pieces of the lock in his hand I could see the calluses of a working man's hands. I had noticed that Scorch's hands did not have long nails and they did not have tobacco stained fingers because unlike many of the local men, he didn't smoke. He rotated the lock in his hand.

"This piece has come loose." I said, holding up the brass bar.

"Looks like today is as good as any day for you to learn to solder," Scorchy said.

Ah...family honor! The day Cal fixed the lock for Holly and she was forever in his debt...*plus* getting to learn a new skill!

"Looks oriental. A pretty piece of work."

"It's from China. Mom and Dad brought it back."

"Ahhhhh soooo!" Scorchy's voice raised a bit, mimicking the sound of a Hollywood Chinaman as he played around. "My buddy Ace was in China for a while. He had quite the time of it over there."

Scorchy had worked for Ace at his motorcycle shop in southern California after he got out of the Army. After all of Scorchy's stories, I was starting to feel like I knew Ace. Bits of his wisdom found their way into Scorch's vocabulary, usually prefaced by, "Like Ace used to say..." Sometimes the stories worked their way into full blown sagas of his life and times. I watched Scorchy carefully for the signs.

His seat seated himself on the on the work bench while he looked at the Chinese inscriptions on the lock. His left foot rose from the floor and the heel of his engineer boot hooked onto the lower table shelf. Scorchy glance went from the lock to the window, which was permanently grimy, and then back at me. I pulled up a crate. Yep...a story was coming.

"Kid, you ever heard of the AVG? The American Volunteer Group?"

I shook my head in the negative.

"The Flying Tigers?"

A light bulb clicked on in my head. Yes! I had seen that movie with John Wayne in it on TV! "Yeah! I saw that on TV. They had tiger jaws painted on their P40 Warhawk fighter planes."

Classic Aurora P-40 Warhawk "Flying Tiger" model kit.

I had built that plane as a plastic kit when I was younger. It was an olive-colored, Aurora plastic kit that came in a box with a painting of the plane sweeping down on a Jap Zero with its guns blazing. Like most of my models, it was a quick build. Cement frosted canopy, fingerprints embedded in the finish...the tiger mouth decals had been difficult, but not as hard as the two eyes that stuck to my fingers! Neither decals, nor glue, ever seemed to dry quickly enough. The motor roared to life inside my head as my lethal new bird of prey revved its motor, prop spinning at near invisibility under my breath (a dab of Vaseline worked wonders!). The .50 caliber machine guns embedded in the molded wings waited longingly to send a stream of lead towards the enemy, tracers piercing the Zeros in my mind's eye. It was a fifty-fifty chance that a fresh model would make it to battle without loss of a landing strut, elevator or wing. Sadly, my "air force" had long since been lost in backyard or vacant lot combat. An old man of twelve, I reflected fondly on my youth.

"Ace had been an Army Air Corps mechanic

in the early thirties," Scorchy began. "From the start he was known as a wrench who could fix anything, and most times better than it had been new. While he was at Maxwell Field in Alabama, Ace started working on cars and motorcycles for his buddies after duty hours for extra pocket money. The cars and bikes he worked on tended to be a bit faster than the others and so word got around...especially when a couple of federal agents inquired as to his connection to some moonshine bootleggers that were just too lucky outrunnin' the law. Ace's commanding officer was *not* happy with having the Feds nosing around his outfit."

Scorch set the lock pieces on the bench, freeing both hands for storytelling.

"So anyway, Ace got asked to 'volunteer' to look at a few pursuit fighter engines that were set to be used for a new demonstration team that was about to tour America at fairs and air shows. Like all the other motors he touched, these radial fighter engines just came out faster. Faster and stronger was just what the leader of that group, Captain Claire Lee Chennault, wanted. He saw to it that Ace became the ground crew for the 'Three Men on a Flying Trapeze' as the group was called. Ace took over a truck loaded with spare parts and tools that was always up front at the next airfield when the team arrived. That lasted till around 1936, when the Army decided that fast bombers were the way of the future. The group disbanded and Chennault retired.

Faced with going back to regular mechanic duties after his six year hitch was up, Ace got out."

"Three Men on the Flying Trapeze" aerobatic team formed by Captain Claire L. Chennault. Chennault expected the impossible from the team and the aircraft. Ace's ability with engines made the team's performance outstanding. They flew in front of more than 50,000 people at 50 different shows.

Scorchy paused, which allowed me to ask, "Did the Feds come after him?" I was hoping for a bit of a gangster story...maybe with a bit of shootin' thrown in.

"Actually, they were waitin' for him when he walked out in civy clothing," Scorchy said. "They wanted Ace to remember that they knew he'd done some work for the wrong kind of guys and that he could set that right by doin' the country a favor. They wanted him to work for one of the major moonshiners down south who they knew would want him for a mechanic. They wanted information and for someone to do sabotage on the bootlegger's hopped-up sedans. But in the 1930s, the life of crime was pretty well documented in the movies and that was enough for Ace to know he wanted nothin' to do with that."

"He told the agents he'd give the offer some thought, but on his first night out of the Army he wanted to go blow some dough on some good times. They warned him not to leave town, gave him a number written inside a match book cover, and told him to call when his head was clear. Instead of tying one on, though, Ace jumped the first westbound freight train."

I must have shifted on the wooden crate, a loose nail squeaked and the sound reminded me of the freight train that morning. Where were those men going?

"No stranger to the boxcar and the hobo jungle, after a brief and frustrating stop in Arkansas, Ace walked out of the Los Angeles freight yard a week later."

"In LA, his Army experience and questions about work as a hop-up mechanic for air racers took him to Hughes Aviation in Culver City. Howard Hughes was known for fast everything, from planes to...well...*everything.* He was working on being the 'fastest man on the planet' and Hughes flew what he built. Ace could talk the talk when he looked at their power plants and so he was told to walk the walk. In a few weeks he was immersed in the projects."

The story was taking an unexpected turn. Working for bootleggers would have been much more adventuresome and I wondered how all this was going to work its way back to the Flying Tigers.

"In 1941, some major events changed everything for Ace. Never able to get enough of hopping up motors, Ace was back to working on motorcycles and cars. Fast cars and bikes were starting to be a big deal in California and there were guys with money who wanted to go fast. Ace had a menu he used to dial in your power plant for whatever price you could or would pay. Workin' out of a garage and using the machine shop at Hughes, his name eventually made its way all the way back to the long ears of the law he had spurned years prior. About that time, Ace also heard from a couple of young Army pilots he tuned bikes for that there was a mercenary air force being formed to fight the Japs in China. As luck would have it, that air force was being commanded by an old Army barnstormer...*Claire Chennault.*"

Howard Hughes, shown here in a Time Magazine cover, produced extreme aircraft. Officially the fastest man in the world, flying one of his own aircraft, Hughes recognized talent in the young Ace Murphy and footed his trip to China to join the American Volunteer Group or "Flying Tigers".

"Howard Hughes understood rebels. He was one himself, after all. Not wanting Ace to suffer at the Fed's hands for his genius with motors, but also not wanting to buck the contracts he saw coming from Washington when war started with Japan, he came up with a solution. Next thing you know, Ace found himself on leave from Hughes Aircraft and on a ship to China with a big wad of cash in his pocket. Hughes called it an investment. Ace was to go to work for the AVG, learn about what was happening in real combat, and when the contract was over come home to Hughes with all he learned to help build the fastest fighter aircraft ever seen."

"The freighter docked at Rangoon, that is in Burma, and Ace tracked down the Americans at a place called Toungoo. He went right to Chennault and volunteered. Of course, he was accepted right away and put to work on the aircraft that were arriving from the USA. There was no lack of work as the mix of Army, Navy, Marine and civilian pilots all had to learn to fly the P40. Some landings being harder than others, this is when Ace got his name. Working through the night, pushing crews and jumping from one P40 to another, he was able to get five wrecks in the air at dawn the next morning. Chennault was on the runway and walked up to him. Shaking his hand, he said, 'Good job, Ace,' and the name stuck."

In my mind there was a disconnect. Ace wasn't always Ace? I could relate, since "Cal" was a nickname, a compilation of the first letters of my name: Cyrus Albert Lee. In the Army years later, I went from Cal to Lee overnight and to those who knew me well enough to look at my papers or ask, I became Cyrus. There wasn't much teasing about names in the Army. Most guys had the same first name... *Private.*

"What is his real name?" I asked.

"Don't know," Scorchy replied. "He never told me. Everything I ever saw had Ace on it."

"Must have gotten him a lot of teasing," I muttered.

"Think his real name got him a lot of trouble. It was easier to leave it in China." Scorchy then slid down off the table. "Kid, we need to get to work. Go over to the bench and get out that propane torch and solder so we can fix this and keep your kid sister out of trouble."

Heat, flux, solder, and ability are what it takes. I had three of the four. The ability was lacking, but finally the detached bar stood in place and the key could push it open again. It was shop policy to send stuff back like new so Scorch wanted to polish the brass casing, but I explained it would not match, best left dull.

"Ace used to say that the best job is the one unseen," Scorchy said. "Like it was never needed."

I guess Ace had done some work for his sister, too!

Do What Ya Do Do Well Boy

The falling down fence next to old orchard. The "Kid" decided to tear it down early in the morning to surprise his folks…it didn't go well.

Locked out!

I rattled the brass padlock that kept "alleyrats" out of the back of the shop. Then, cruising along the wall all the way out to the street, I checked the front door handle. Locked as well. Figuring Scorchy must be at breakfast at the diner, I stepped out onto the street.

Head down, not looking to the right or left, my mind was back home. A few steps into the street I was rocked back on my heels by the blast of a pickup truck horn.

"Hey! Watch where you're goin'!" And then, barely loud enough for my ears to hear, *"Stupid kid!"*

A time would come, when I was older, when I would have turned the situation back on the guy. At twelve years old, though, I knew I was out of my league.

Looking both ways to make sure the road was clear this time, I headed across the town's main street, hopped the little irrigation ditch, and walked up to the glass door of the diner. The door swung in. No danger of getting plowed while I checked the scene inside.

Peering through the glass, I could see that the place was about half-full. Mostly the same old guys with their coffee and smokes...pipes or cigarettes mostly. At the time Dad smoked a little and my uncle smoked regularly, but I wasn't accustomed to that, or many other adult vices. While I thought it would be cool to smoke, walking into a smoke-filled room always made me think twice. Scorchy was sitting at the counter with Wanda standing nearby. They were talking. Not much of a surprise there. Everyone could see she had taken to Scorchy right off the first morning he had walked in.

Back then, I looked at Wanda in different ways, but mostly the way a kid looks at things. She often put in extra lunch or pie for me when I was "workin' with Scorchy, so on that count she was great. But every boy in town knew she was probably divorced, and that (you'd hear the older guys say) she was "not bad looking" in that older sort of way that is hard to explain as a preteen. You know something's happenin' in your mind and body, but you're not ready for it. Least I wasn't, but then I was behind a lot of my classmates — farm boys who were growing hair and whose voices were already changing — but mostly I saw Wanda as competition for Scorchy's attention. Scorchy and I had "work" to do. Then there was the '53. Just who needed girls when he had that?!

I finally pushed the diner door and it opened with a slight scrape from all the boot grit worn into the floor. Every head in the place turned towards the sound. Seeing me at the door, they all went back to chores of smokin,' sippin,' eatin,' or jawin.' Everyone except Scorchy.

"Hey, Kid! You early or am I late?" Scorchy said with a slight smile.

"Nah, I'm early," I replied. "Wonderin' if you needed any help today?"

Was that a bit of a dark look from Wanda? Rainin' and pourin' is how the day was goin' for me.

"Haven't lined out the work yet for today, anybody waitin'?"

I shook my head. There was no need to rush.

"Kid, well then you better have a piece of pie and a milk before we get to it." Scorchy always seemed to have a couple quarters, a dime or nickel in his pocket nowadays as more farm work and other jobs makin' stuff for folks had appeared. Scorch put a quarter on the counter and Wanda delivered the apple pie and cold milk.

"Thank you, ma'am!"

"It's Wanda," she replied.

"Thank you, Miss Wanda! Thank you, Scorchy!" I said, and then I dove into the pie and milk.

I'd spent the last four years in Texas before we moved up to Montana. Polite was required in Texas, and I got paddled regularly for talking out of turn, not ma'amin,' noy sir'in,' or forgetting to let the girls go first. I knew polite. I tried to mind my own business while Wanda and Scorchy continued their conversation. There was something happening in a neighboring town over the weekend. Between chews I heard something that sounded like, "take your bike down," and I popped out of my self-imposed solitary state.

"You gettin' the panhead out, Scorchy?"

Was it my tone? Was it my look? Maybe it was my enthusiasm? I don't know, but again, every head in the place turned to look first at me, then at Scorchy, and then at Wanda and back at me before returning to what they'd been doing. Wanda looked a bit flushed, with a slight red tinge on her ears. Scorch's eyes kinda sparkled and he had just a smidgin' of a grin. He glanced over at Wanda, whose blush was fading, and then gave me a very clear "mind your own biz, kid" look and I could very clearly feel the divide between adult and kid.

I stood up to leave, staring at the floor. "Thank you for the pie," I managed to say in a whisper breathed at the floor. I turned and made my way to the front door. The handle felt heavy in my hand.

"Hey, Kid!"

I turned back towards Scorchy and Wanda just in time to see a key already on its way to me in a long slow arch. Again, the heads turned to watch. Everyone knew I couldn't catch. My dad knew, every kid knew, everyone in the whole damn town knew...and I thought Scorchy knew. I reached for it, choked, and missed like always. The key hit the floor and I could hear a snicker or two as I bent to pick it up.

"Go ahead and open up, get the lights on," Scorchy said. "I left her hard last night, so if you could get the tools back in place and the main bench cleared up that would be aces. I'll be along in a bit."

"Yes, sir," I managed, feeling like my wind had been knocked out a bit. I heard someone at one of the tables mutter what sounded like, "Some kinda..." A quick, hard glance from Scorchy froze that voice mid-syllable.

Stepping into the street, I was hating Wanda.

I unlocked the back door, reached in, and turned on the light switch. A couple of the bare bulbs overhead came to life. Years of fire and work had blackened the shop walls until they sucked in most of what the bulbs put out.

Over by the forge there was a pull string lamp with fluorescent tubes. I pulled the string and they flickered to life. Their chatter bounced off the only reflective mass in the shop, the panhead motorcycle. Uncovered and sitting on a few blocks of wood, she was straight and square. The back wheel was off and lay nearby. The glow of the chrome and leaping orange flames beckoned me and my thoughts began to drift.

I pulled myself back and continued with my light strings and switches. I went over to the bench and started picking up tools and putting them away. What was Scorchy doing with the bike? My mind churned as I put smaller pieces of scrap metal into a bin and put the larger pieces onto a rack.

Was it broken?

Wipe down the benches...

Was he leavin'?

Start sweeping the floor around the benches and get the sweepins into the trash can that's gettin' full.

My eyes adjusted to the dim lamp glow. Looking back at the bike I noticed a pad was resting on the rear fender. That meant only one thing...Scorchy was going to be giving someone a ride. I cranked up on the cleanup. Things were looking up!

I had awakened at 5:00 AM that morning determined I was going to get a job done. Between the house and the hay field was an old apple orchard and an old, broken down barbwire fence. Rotten posts and loose wires made it a danger to my sisters who played in the yard. Mom had complained about it, so I decided to take action.

I had never worked with barbwire before, but I had rolled up a rope or two, how could it be different?

Quietly, I exited the house and went over to an old red railroad boxcar that had been set on a foundation of railroad ties by the barn some time before we bought the place. We called it "the box car" and it held our tools. At night, our dog slept there. Fritz bounded out as I slid the door open. Like all dogs, Fritz was always ready for whatever adventure I might have in mind.

Claw hammer, pliers, and baseball gloves were the tools I selected. I went over to the first fence pole and put the claw under the wire and pulled at the first horseshoe-shaped fencing staple. The wood was old and it came out easily. I was surprised by the spring in the slack wire. I loosened the top strand for the full length of the fence ending with what seemed to be a nearly living fifty foot piece of wire. It seemed to jump when I touched it. I put on the baseball gloves and began coiling. With each new coil I found the going harder as the wire strained to escape, writhing, snatching the grass and weeds as I pulled it along. By the time my mom was up making coffee, I had managed to finish one strand of wire, a rough bulging mass subdued with bailing twine.

My father came out to see what I was doing and told me to stop. He went back inside and I waited for an eternity until he came out in work clothes. He explained that I had coiled the wire wrong, and that there was a procedure for rolling the wire so that the barbs caught and held the strands in place as they coiled. He put on a pair of heavy gloves and then cut the twine holding my coil together.

It exploded.

My father was not a cusser, and limited himself to hell and damn. He showed me my error and how to get it "ship shape." The heavy work gloves in place of the baseball mitts were a huge improvement, and the way he did it was neater and much more efficient. Then, I was told to basically shove off.

Dad had stuff on his mind, and he had not

wanted to do this project. At least not this morning, but my attempt had created a chore that he now had to finish. While I might have had good intentions, I had inserted myself into an equation that was not mine to solve.

The shop's arc welder that Scorchy used to turn pipe into a set of handrails for Mr. Lee.

Scorchy came into the shop about a half hour after I had arrived and started cleaning up.

"Time to get to work," he said as he surveyed my work. "Looks ready to go."

He walked over to the electric welder. The welder was more or less a big box that took 220 volt electricity out of the wall and turned it into a blazing jolt that could fuse steel. The whole rig was mounted on wheels, like a cart, with a handle. Scorchy grabbed the handle and dragged it towards the bench. "Get your gloves off the bench," Scorchy said. "Right behind you are some poles. Pass the first one up here. Job number one today is a set of hand rails for some steps."

Settling into "work," I responded to Scorchy's direction: "bring this...hold here...chalk this line..." while Scorchy cut, shaped, welded, and ground what were really little more that scrap and junk metal. A couple of hours later, they had been transformed into two perfect hand rails ready to be painted, set in concrete, and used to steady someone on their steps.

We worked together to clear a space next to the door where we stood the railings up so they would be easy to load in the customer's truck. Several small pieces of usable scrap were left over.

"Stack those over by the railings so the customer can take 'em if he wants." Scorchy always did a good job of planning how he would use his raw materials, and he a great eye for detail. I did as he asked and then started to sweep up the bits left on the floor.

"Hey, Kid!" Scorchy said. "When you got that, I've got another job for ya!" He handed me some loose change and a piece of paper. "Run over to Wanda's...the diner...and call the number on this invoice and let the customer know we got his job done. Then use what's left over for sodas over at the IGA. You fly, I'll buy. Coke for me!"

I swept the dust pile into the flat-nosed, broken handled shovel, and took it out to the garbage. Swinging back through, I put the shovel away and picked up the empty bottles from our last break to take with me. Going back to the diner to make a phone call and asking Wanda for anything was not on my plate of things I wanted to do. I was still jealous of her gettin' ideas about Scorchy and the '53.

"A job ain't always fun, that's when it's work!" Scorchy had said once. Well this wasn't really "work," but it was a job to do. Looking both ways, I walked to the other side of Main Street, hopped the ditch, and used my spare hand to open the diner door.

The place was empty, but would fill up some once lunch started. Wanda was checking tables: wiping them down with a damp cloth, adding paper napkins, checking the salt shakers, catsup, and mustard. It seemed the pepper never got empty. She turned to look at the sound of the door opening. Her look had gone back to being friendly. "Hi, Kid," Wanda said. My new moniker had started to spread.

"Scorchy sent me to call a customer to pick up some work," I said. "Can I use the phone?" I was polite but cool. I got a "sure, go ahead" in reply as Wanda continued her table rounds.

The phone was on the wall, a black pay job. I could reach it without standing on a stool or box, which made me feel taller and older. Setting the empties on the floor, I cradled the phone on my shoulder and dropped a dime into the slot and got a dial tone. I flipped open the invoice and knew the number right away, it was *my* house.

Mom answered the phone on the third ring. "Lee residence, can I help you?" My "Mrs. Lee, your two step railings are finished." was met with, "Is that you, Cal? Are you ok?"

My business presence deflated, I acknowledged that, indeed, it was me and that I was indeed fine and that WE — Scorchy and I — had just finished the railings and Mr. Black wanted to let Dad know so he could come pick them up. The bill was $8.50 which was itemized into two hours of labor and a welding rod. Mom then let me know that Dad would pick them up at the end of the day...and was I coming home for lunch?

Hanging up the phone I stuck my finger into the coin return on the bottom and got my dime back. I noticed Wanda was sitting on a chair, legs crossed tight inside her skirt. "Thanks for letting me use the phone," I said.

Touching up her lipstick using a hand compact mirror, she puckered her lips and then made a little kissing sound. "You bet, Kid. Tell Scorchy I have some leftover pork roast and some gravy that should be eaten."

Again, I noticed the legs, the lips, and still heard the kiss. Slightly light-headed, I walked out the door only to get a few steps before remembering to go back and get the empty Coke bottles.

Scorchy was laying some large pieces of steel on the cutting table when I got back to the shop.

"Ah, nothing for the thirst like a cold Coke unless it is hot coffee!" He snapped off the tops on the table handing one over.

Several drinks into mine I reported that Wanda had some food she was going to throw away if Scorch didn't eat it. Then I told him that the customer for the railings was my own father.

Scorchy looked at his Coke, made a happy, appreciative sound that expressed all the joy it seemed to bring him. "Yep, I know. Be sure you're here to help load him out."

I didn't really know how to bring up the legs, skirt, lips, and kiss sound. I finished up my Coke and after Scorchy was done with his, we worked till noon. Expected home, I took off at a trot for lunch. After a hot bowl of Spaghetti-O's, a glass of milk, and some peaches from a big can, I was again back up town to the shop. The north bound freight train was just moving past the crossing on River Road as I arrived. I flipped the brakeman in the caboose a wave. He made a friendly wave back.

Scorchy was working as I slumped through the door. He was just finishing a cut and was turning off the torch. He flipped up his goggles at my approach.

"Kid, you're lookin' a little down in the chops. Have a seat on the bench. What's givin' you the hangdog look?"

Boosting myself up on the bench I relayed the story of my morning with the fence. My thoughts about Wanda I kept to myself.

"Kid," he said. "Your old man...I mean your dad...is going through some changes in his life. He's still young and he is leaving behind a job that's pretty much all he knows. Uncle Sam is going to pay him a retirement. I'm sure as an officer that's okay money. He won't need to worry much, but he's gonna have to find his way again. A lot of men get lost in this time of life. You're going to think some of the lost-ness is your fault. He may even say stuff to you that I'm sure he'll hate later. But I've seen a fair share of good and bad, and I know bums. Your dad is no bum. He's put a lot of stuff in front of his own well-being, both people and things. Your mom and you kids are a big part of that. Just remember there's a good man there. Believe me, I had a hardass for an old man, too. I shoulda, coulda, listened and learned more. Maybe I learned some anyway. Like Ace would say, 'It's all the same tune just a new verse.' Gonna be the same for you someday.

Want more closeness with your own kid some-day...you gotta be the one sayin' I love you a little more."

Scorch ran a gloved hand across his face and there was a bit of a wet smear in the corner of his eye. He pulled the goggles back down and re-lit the torch.

Cleanup had started when my dad finally showed up. Scorchy greeted him with, "After-noon, Mr. Lee, would you like the Kid to pull your truck around back while you wait and we'll load your railings?"

The kid in question was me, of course, and I was not of legal age to drive (not that it stopped any other boy working for someone in town). I had some bootleg time in our truck out in the field, driving with Dad in the back as we moved from ditch to ditch so he could set the heavy can-vas irrigation dams that directed the flooding of the fields, but that was first gear going in a straight line. This was going to require reverse, backing up, traffic, signals, and maybe second gear! Most of me hoped Dad would say no, that he'd do it.

"Sure, keys are in it," my dad said, much to my surprise. "Let me take care of the bill."

"Hey, Kid! Pull Mr. Lee's truck around back so we can load him up."

I set down the broom and squared my shoul-ders. "Right, Scorchy."

As I walked up front, Dad was studiously examining some old saw blades. He seemed wholly entranced, "Keys are in it," he seemed to tell the saw blades.

Our tan-colored International pickup squatted out front on Main Street, the big front grill grinning at me as if to say, "Think you can handle all *this?*" I took my place behind the wheel, pushed in the clutch, and turned the key, feeling the motor start. I pushed the gear shift into reverse and began to let out the clutch.

The Lee family pick-up — an International Harvester truck, it was heavy duty in every way. The Kid had to use the manual transmission to back up and get it behind the shop to load out his dad's handrails.

"Get your head out of the cockpit!" I clearly heard Dad yell in my head as I punched the clutch back in and remembered to crane my neck left, right, and left again to check for traffic. I let a car go by and then Main Street was mercifully empty. The truck began to jerk backwards as the clutch plate bit the flywheel. By the time I got it back in, I was in the middle of the street.

First gear and clutch again. Not bad, as I was now going forward and first gear is familiar to me. I crawl up Main Street to First Avenue. I remembered to signal and turned left, straightening out just in time to turn left again down the alley. Pushing the clutch in a final time, I braked behind the shop and turned off the key, letting the clutch back out as the engine rumbled and died. Silence as several tons lifted from my shoulders. I did it! I made it! I glanced around. Did any other kids see me?!

Scrochy was watching from the shop door. "OK, Kid, let's get 'em loaded!" he called out.

I think I floated from the truck cab and through the back door before falling in behind Scorchy. We picked up the first rail together, putting it nice and easy into the truck bed. Then the second one, just as easy.

I turned to see Dad standing back in the shop, watching us. "Well, thanks fellows," he said. "Those look really well made. Good job."

He was looking right at me.

Scorchy Meets the King

Sergeant Elvis Presley and a mechanic look at damage to a jeep. Could this be independent, historical proof of the late night meeting of the King and Scorchy?

Scorchy's past came out in bits and pieces, usually prompted by some event. Like nearly every day of that summer, I wandered into the shop to "work" with the drifter-biker-come-blacksmith, Scorchy Black. Today my job was to move scraps from a dump barrel into the trash can if they didn't spec out, or to the storage rack if they did.

"Hey, Kid, make sure you put the pointy ends towards the wall," Scorchy said. "Don't need any of the alleyrats bangin' into 'em and come whinin' to me."

The "alleyrats" were a group of boys who hung out in the back of Muller's Bar and wandered behind the grocery store and the shop, always on the lookout for anything not locked down. Scorchy was a quick judge of character and if he got a bad vibe about someone, that vibe stuck until either proved or proved wrong. In time I learned that Scorchy was rarely wrong, even about some of my stuff.

A small radio, found on top of a trashcan on one of Scorchy's walks, now played during shop hours. A loose connection caused the reception to noisily cut on and off each time a loud note jiggled it. KOOK was the local AM station and played rock 'n roll that came in pretty clear at night but, was scratchy during the day. Elvis's new hit "Crying in the Chapel" came on as I hauled a load out to the trash. When I returned, I noticed Scorchy with his foot up on a box, toe tappin' to the beat. His face turned towards the radio, for a second he seemed to be entranced as if lost in a dream.

I propped one of my Chuck Taylors on a box and mimicked Scorchy's stance, with my left elbow on my knee and my right arm over it. I tried to match the detached, ever so slight bob of his head. Less than two minutes later, the DJ's voice told us it was Elvis Presley, the King of Rock and Roll, and he rolled into the station ID. A chorus of harmonizing voiced reminded us we were listing to *"Kaaaaaaay-Ooooo-Ooooo-Kaaaaaaaaaaay in Billlllinggggsss."* Scorchy shook himself out of his trance and looked over at me.

A DJ at KOOK, broadcasting from Billings, reads a spot. He has a 45 cued on the turntable.

"He's pretty good, huh Kid?"

"He sure is! The best for sure!" I fired back like an answer to a classroom quiz. Really, I didn't think that at all. My budding musical tastes ran more towards the likes of the new band out of Britain, "Herrman and the Hermits," of which I had memorized every song, applying Peter Noone's English accent in what I thought was a most masterful way, certain that no one would be able to tell the difference in a blind test. I had even made my own cardboard Fender electric guitar with Tinker Toys knobs from my toy chest, Marks-a-Lot strings, and colored Crayola crayon red and white. Later in life I acquired a mature, "classic" taste for music, but for now I was a kid and I was aiming to please.

Herman's Hermits' 45 record sleeve for "I'm Henry the Eight, I Am."

"Pulled a jeep off him," Scorchy said.

"Huh?" I replied, not quite comprehending. "You pulled a jeep offa' Elvis? What was Elvis doin' under a jeep?"

Scorchy stood up and stuck a hand into his Levis pocket, pulling out a dime. "It's a good story and we're caught up," He said. The dime flicked from his thumb, through the air, and blessedly into my hands and stayed there. "I'll buy, you fly. I'll have a Coke."

I grabbed the two empty bottles from our last break off the bench and was out the door like a shot on the way to the little IGA down the street. Just inside the front door there was a bright red Coca-Cola machine that had all known flavors of soda pop swimming in ice water. As I passed through the door, a cheery "Afternoon!" from Mrs. Eddy greeted my ears.

"Afternoon, ma'am," I replied in my best Texas polite. I held up the two empty bottles with my fingers like I'd seen Scorchy do it and got a nod of acknowledgement before dropping them into the wooden bottle rack. "Can I have change for the Coke machine?" The sodas in the Coca-Cola machine cost a nickel, so I had to break the dime.

"How's business going with Mr. Black and the blacksmith shop?" Mrs. Eddy asked. "He sure spends a lot of time at the diner. Guess he must like something over there? Hmmm?"

Mrs. Eddy's question floated by as I wrestled with making the choice between an icy Coke, like Scorchy favored, or my own favorite, Dr. Pepper. When I first arrived in Montana, the new soda sensation was Mountain Dew. The cartoon commercials of the hillbilly with his hat blowing off when he took a swig, combined with peer pressure from other local boys, had lured me temporarily into the "Yahoooo!" camp, but now I felt I

Cyrus Lee

needed to make a more adult choice, so I grabbed a Coke.

I might have answered her, but I don't know. I responded to "Here's your change" with "Thank you, ma'am" as I walked over to the red and white treasure chest. I opened the lid. Fresh ice floated in the water filled the soda bottles. You pushed a nickel into the coin slot and when you heard the coin hit the bottom of the coin-box, you could slide your bottle of Coke down the rails that held them in place just below the caps. At the end of the rails you maneuvered the bottle through a trap door arrangement and then pulled it out with a mechanical "ker-chunk!" Experience with older boys who thought it was funny to cheat a kid out of his soda money by reaching in and pulling the door up too early had taught me to make sure my pop was in the trap door before I fed my money into the coin slot. Even though I was alone, I followed that procedure as I pulled each Coke from the machine. The icy glass bottles quickly condensed with little rivulets of ice water as I headed out the door.

One of the great things about getting a Coke for Scorchy was watching him open it. He'd hold the cap against the edge of the metal shop table top and snap down on it with the heel of his palm and the top would fly off. Just like Tony and Riff in West Side Story, he would then hand me the first one. I had tried this maneuver on my own in private on several surfaces at home. The results were always less than satisfactory.

90

The Coke machine from the IGA store showing
the selection rack, bottle release and coin box.

Scorchy settled on the table and took a slow swig. He always acted like it was the first time he had ever tasted a soda, gazing appreciatively at the bottle and emitted a contented "Ahh....." One of Scorchy's stories was coming. I pulled up a box and tuned in.

"I turned 18 in 1956," he began, "which was just after the Korean War. I had registered with the draft and I figured if I joined I might get a better job, maybe something I could learn from. I signed on for a four year hitch. A 63C, or a General Vehicle Repairman, is what I became after I went to basic training. I spent a couple of years down in Texas at Fort Hood and then I was shipped out to Germany and ended up at Coleman Kaserne, or I should say barracks or base. In the little town of Gelnhausen, I was in Headquarters Company, 2nd Battalion, 48th Infantry Battalion part of the motor pool. I don't know why I ended up there 'cause most of the vehicles were armored personnel carriers, like a tank that carries a squad of soldiers. Yet it turned out pretty good for me. I had some good times in town, worked hard and got along with my sergeants. That's where I learned to weld and work metal, as well as mechanic work on engines, transmissions and other stuff."

Years later I'd understand a lot of Scorchy was describing on a first hand basis, but in 1965 I was the son of retired navy officer and I had no clue about military life beyond World War II history and what navy pilots said to their families when they came home at night. I took a pull off my Coke, gazed appreciatively at the bottle, and emitted a long "ahhhh...." of my own.

"About a month after I was in garrison," Scorchy continued. "I got my Army driver's license so I could drive the various vehicles in the motor pool, which is like a parking lot where the Army keeps vehicles till you use 'em. I got so I could drive 'em all, from the jeep to the M59 armored personnel carrier, called 'em APC's for short. Most of all I drove the M37 — that's like a big pickup truck — carrying tools, parts, supplies. Right off the bat I found out that a GI who did what he was told and did it well would get more work than those who didn't. But I also figured out pretty quick you got more freedom as well and found myself driving to different Kasernes, or bases, to drop off broken parts or pick up spares, equipment, paperwork, and things like that. I'd always have a little time to stop by the snack bar for a burger if I wanted, or to check out the Stars & Stripes bookstore as long as I was back to G-town in time to unload and get some other work done. Sometimes I'd drive one of the NCOs — sergeants — or officers on a trip and get to miss some of the BS on base. I also got to see a lot of the country that way."

M37 Dodge Truck — Scorchy was driving an M37 like this the night he met Sgt. Presley.

Scorchy took another pull off his Coke while he paused. "Everyone in the USA, heck, the *world*, knew that Elvis was in the Army in Germany. In fact, he was in 3rd Armored like me, up in Friedberg at Ray Barracks in a tank unit. He wasn't a tread-head, but a jeep driver in the Scout Section. He soldiered pretty much like everyone else, but he had a place off post to live. It was the winter of '59 and 2-48 had deployed to Wildflecken. Wildflecken is a training area, a place a whole outfit can go do stuff you can't do back in garrison. We went to different training areas, but Wildflecken was probably the one most guys liked least. Guys called it "Wildchicken" or worse. The post is up on top of a mountain and sometimes you can't see it when the clouds are hanging low. In winter, there is always snow up there. Windy...cold as the dickens, but it was closer to G-town than Graf or Hohenfels, the other big training areas we'd go to. So it was not unusual for somebody to need something from back on the post, so I'd find myself driving back and forth a few times. Nice, as it broke up the routine of the 45 days we'd be up there."

Scorchy's military home in Germany, Coleman Kaserne, near Gelnhausen. The motor pool soldiers from 2/48 Infantry lived in the barracks at the top right of photo and worked in the motor pool located in the single story buildings center left of the photo.

Scorchy set the Coke down on the table for a moment, deep in thought...then picked it back up and took a swig before carrying on.

"German winters are dark. Dawn comes late and evenings early. When you are out in the forest, it gets really black. Driving down the B-40, the German highway to Fulda and the West and East German border that marks the beginning of Iron Curtain, you swing south to Wildflecken. While you are on the Bundesstraße or on post you have your headlights on. The army calls it 'white light,' but soon as you hit the tank- trails or the roads to the training sites you have to go to 'blackout drive' which means you're drivin' in the dark and it's pitch black dark. They figure in combat you can't be lightin' up the place so the enemy sees ya, so you better learn to drive in the dark. All the blackout drive does is mark your vehicle so when you are near other vehicles they can spot you...and I mean close!"

Wildflecken in winter — Snow blankets the main post at Wildflecken Training Area. The deep snow and limited visibility could come on quickly as Scorchy and Elvis learned that night.

"I was runnin' late because the parts I was bringing back had taken me longer to get than what it should, but the NCO in the rear was good to go with a time out that covered me for hot chow in the mess hall. With a full tank of fuel and a thermos of coffee, I hit the road and hot footed it all the way to Wildflecken as I wasn't in a convoy. It was late when I got on post and later still when I got on the tank-trail to Bivouac Area Kilo, the mountain top where 2-48's infantry companies were dug in and camouflaged, practicing defense. I knew the first guards were getting posted. The cold was coming down and the sky was crystal clear with the stars right on top of your head. The moon was bright which helped keep me on the road."

I edged up on my box, getting sucked in now.

"Two small red lights glowed softly on the dash of the truck. I always made sure my truck heater worked well, so I drove without gloves, my hands devil-red in the glow. It's easy to get distracted while you drive along at a walking pace, so I was humming Elvis's 'Need Your Love Tonight.' I had heard it on AFN — the American Forces Network — the radio all GI's listened to. I wondered how Elvis was recording songs while he was in the Army. Later I found out he recorded them on leave before he went overseas."

"Second gear in four wheel high kept the M37 crawling along at a nice even pace. I'd mastered the skill of unauthorized single-hand steering so

I could sip on my thermos cup of coffee, your typical mess hall brew of new grounds and water on top of old. The tank trail started to dip a bit and in the moonlight I could see a left hand turn coming up. I pushed in the hand throttle on the dash and let my right foot take over."

"As I started around the turn I could feel a slight slip on the ice. Not a big deal...just take it slow. The trails are all cambered so they drift off to either side into a barrow pit on the sides and as I came round the turn I spotted the rear end of a jeep, the nose down in the ditch. Some poor GI was going to have to hoof it and was gonna take some serious flak for goin' too fast and putting her in the ditch. I was goin' to just keep drivin' but that little voice ya' get in the back of your head quipped, 'Stop and take a look.'"

M-60 tank after sliding off a tank trail near Bivowac Area Kilo at the Wildflecken Training Area. Elvis could have slid off the same corner.

"I pushed in the clutch and gingerly braked the M37 to a stop at the side of the trail. My Army boots slid on the ice as got out of the cab. Boy, it was cold, below freezing...and then, crystal clear, I hear this cry, *'Help! I'm under the jeep! Hel-l-l-p!'*"

Scorchy's voice changes to mimic the helpless GI and he's pretty darned good at it. I'm so caught up that I haven't taken a swig of Coke in a long while.

"I sound off with *'I'm commin'!'* and I grab my bent neck flashlight out of the M37 cab. I switch it on and its red light flows over the trail as I head for the jeep. Towards the front, I can see legs. *'I'm here, buddy!'* I yell, *'I'll get you out!'* I set the light down with the beam on the guy's legs and grab hold, pulling while he shouts, *'I'm stuck! You gotta get it off me!'*"

"He's really stuck. I take a quick look in the jeep and spot C-Ration boxes. *'Hold on!'* I tell him, *'I'm getting' a breaker bar outa my truck!'* After I grab the bar, I imagine my old boss, Ace Murphy, sayin' 'Careful Kid, work safe. I don't give no time off for stupid!' So I check to see if the jeep is in gear or the handbrake is set before I shove the stick forward and rip back the brake handle."

"I grab a box of C-Rations and set it on the ground close to the jeep. C-Ration boxes are hard and the cans inside will provide a good fulcrum for my bar. You know what a fulcrum is, Kid? That basic engineering..."

I nod in the affirmative. We studied that in math, though I thought that a fulcrum was pointed on top. Maybe that's a Greek one, but if Scorchy says a box works I'm not sayin' a word. I mean, heck...*he's savin' Elvis!*

"I stick the bar under the edge of the jeep body and add a little pressure. *'Okay,'* I holler, *'I'm gonna lift! Scoot yourself out!'* I hear an 'Okay' from under the jeep and then throw all my weight against the bar. Jeeps ain't all that heavy, so up she goes. I hear shuffling' and then the guy says, *'I'm out!'* I set the jeep back down. The top box of C's is dented."

A box of C-Rations. Scorchy used several of these boxes to make a fulcrum to lift the Jeep off of Elvis.

"'You ok, buddy?' I ask the soldier as he struggles to get upright. 'Yes, sir,' he says, 'I sure am...thanks to you!' There's something familiar about his voice as I retrieve my flashlight. 'Let me check you out, buddy.' I turn the flashlight towards him and the red light shines on a face that I've seen on magazine covers. His white nametape is smeared with grease but reads

'PRESLEY.'"

"I remember back when I'd messed up a job at Ace's. It had been a stupid move on my part, thinking I could carry more than I could really balance and see to navigate the shop floor. I tripped on a step and it all hit the floor. Parts all over. Ace took a look, asked if I was ok, and then just said, 'Clean it up and get back to work.' Later, after quitin' time, he sat me down and told me I needed to be careful and that I'd have to make up for the damaged goods. I told him I'd make good. He said he knew I would. Much later I asked him how come he hadn't chewed me out and he told me he knew that I knew I had been wrong and since I kept cool, so did he. 'A man needs to respect another man, even when he makes a mistake. Treat folks like you want to be treated.'"

"Presley was no kid at this point and he was a Buck Sergeant, three up on the sleeve of his field jacket. I was a Specialist-5th Class, a rank the Army used to promote you for having skill, not so much for being a leader. Presley was a hard stripe NCO. I kept myself in check, playin' it cool. Respect..."

"'Let's get your jeep out of the ditch, Sarge,' I say. 'I've got a tow cable in the back.' We walked over to the back of my M37 where I started to root for the cable. 'You feelin' alright?' I asked. 'How long you been under there?'"

"'I been there a while,' Evlis replied. 'It was just dusk when I slid off the edge. Figured I could jack the jeep up and get her back on the road...don't know what I was thinking. No sooner got it up when it slid right over the top of me and I was pinned. Boy, when the other guys hear about this...'"

"'Ah, heck,' I told him, 'Stuff happens to everyone. Jeep looks fine. You seem ok, just a little greasy. We'll get her out and then you're on your way. I'm headin' for Kilo, so I'll follow ya to make sure you got no problems. You're gonna have to come up with your own story for bein' late. Say, why don't you go pull that clevis pin and get this end of the cable on.'"

"Presley took the cable and headed back to his jeep. This was not a tough recovery and I knew we'd be out in a minute. The M37 in low four could pull stumps and the jeep popped right out. I had Presley start it up and then asked him if he'd like to warm a minute in the cab. I knew he had to be cold and pretty stiff. 'Got a little mess hall joe here, how 'bout a cup?'"

"As Elvis warmed up a bit he started to get a bit more anxious about getting on the road. Not my place to tell him he should take a few more minutes, so I said something about headin' out and I'd be behind. Presley caught my nametag in the cab light. 'Say, Black, what's your outfit?' he asked. I told him I was in the 2-48 Motor Pool in G-Town, not tough to find. Presley reached for the door handle, opened the door and stepped out. 'Thanks, Black, I owe you one. You don't mind keepin' this between a couple soldiers?'"

"I guess I could've asked for an autograph to prove who I helped, but then who'd that have been for? Just about me. Army's a leveler a lot of times. Instead I just said, 'Sure, Sarge...stuff happens. Glad I was around to help.' And then the King of Rock n' Roll got into his jeep and pulled out. I followed till I got to the Kilo turn off and headed up the road to headquarters to check in.

"Later, just before I left Germany, I got a package in the APO and in it was a greasy field jacket with a note. It said, 'Got back safe and sound. Thanks for the help on the road and keeping it mum! This might be worth something someday...Elvis'"

The M-51 Field Jacket that arrived at Scorchy's APO in Gelnhausen along with note and torn wrapping.

Sunday Late for Meetin'

Dressed in a good shirt and pants, already warm — too warm for school clothes on a summer Sunday — I walked the cracked and broken sidewalk up the road from the house towards town. I had a date...well maybe a duty...well...a job.

At 9:45 every Sunday morning, I rang the steeple bell at the Methodist Church to invite the community to services. The bell had been frozen in its cradle for years and recently repaired. For some reason, I volunteered to be the guy who showed up early to ring it.

Green Beret Staff Sergeant Barry Sadler on the 45 record sleeve of his hit "The Ballad of the Green Berets."

It may have been the thrill of making a huge noise on Sundays as I signaled the fifteen minute warning...then stirred it up again when there was five minutes to go. It may have been that the pastor's sons were pretty cool guys. One was still in high school, seemed to be popular, and actually talked to me now and then, while the other was just out of the Army and a Green Beret. "The Ballad of the Green Beret" by Barry Sadler was a huge hit on Ed Sullivan and the radio. My aunt had bought me the sheet music to it, so I knew all the words. He didn't talk much about the army. He was heading to seminary like his dad before him. And then there was Sandy, a senior, who played the piano and...well...she made me feel good when I was around her.

The highway running south into Wyoming was still. There wasn't a car or truck in sight when I began to hear it...a low, rhythmic, mechanical beat that sounded something like *"potato-potato-potato-potato."* By the time I got into the "canyon" on Main Street formed by the building fronts to either side, the sound was more staccato as it rebounded off the hard surfaces of the buildings. Though it was out of sight, I knew well the sound of Scorchy's '53 panhead. The bike had been parked inside the shop since the day it had brought Scorchy to town. Scorchy had started it, let me sit on it, but I had yet to see it back out in Montana's clear, Big Sky daylight. As I rounded the corner I began sinning.

Sin Number One: I was on the way to ring the church bell, not to hang out with my "boss," Scorchy. I was easily swayed from my clerical duty by lust. Sunlight sparkled off the chrome handle bars, the springs on the front forks, the headlight, and the wheels. The orange red flames seemed to glow and pulse on the black as the bike surged with each stroke of the V-shaped motor. In my mind's eye I was already straddling the seat, hands on the jackhammer grips, ready to roar out of town...

"Hey," a voice said. "Morning, Kid."

Smooth as honey with just hint of husky, Wanda had a voice boys in town would go buy a Coke or a milkshake just to hear...to maybe have her call them "honey."

Sin Number Two: A "carryover sin." I was still not happy about Wanda and all the attention she was paying to Scorchy. Yet, polite is polite, and as I turned, I replied, "Morning, ma'am...Wanda."

I caught a flash of red. A tight red bandana was holding her hair up, pony tail out the back. Her red lipstick was hot and glowing like the bike's flames. Her eyes looked bigger somehow and I noticed she wasn't wearing her waitress dress. I'd never seen her without the waitress dress. Levis stretched over her hips and down her long legs to her ankles where they were cuffed up. She wore a sleeveless shirt with the top three pearl snap buttons undone. I got a hot flash just looking at her.

Figuring out what she was doing there wasn't tough and I added to that Sin Number Three: Being just a little bit jealous of Scorchy. I think I just about had my mouth closed as I started being angry at him for what he was about to do.

"The bike sounds pretty nice, doesn't it?" Wanda asked. She was clever, directing the subject away from the obvious, which was *her*. It occurred to me that I was staring at her on the "pretty nice" part.

"Yes, ma'am, it sure does!"

"It's Wanda, Kid. We've been over that. I'm not your mom or your aunt." Saving me from myself, or just tired of my staring, she slid on a fringed leather jacket. It was a buckskin, Davey Crockett-looking thing, but I don't recall Davey having any fancy silver bits of flash attached to his jacket when he was fighting in Disney's *Alamo*. "So, Kid, what are you up to?"

Fess Parker and Buddy Epson from Walt Disney's Davey Crocket mini-series. When Wanda put on her fringe leather jacket she did not look like Fess Parker.

"I'm going to ring the church bell," I replied. "It's one of my jobs." I'd taken my eyes off her and was now focused on the bike. "Scorchy goin' someplace?"

"He's taking me over to the Wild West Rodeo shindig. I don't know if he's much of a rodeo kind of guy, but there's the parade and other fun stuff."

Sin Number Three climbed a couple of degrees higher, as did my anger at how blind Scorchy was being. Why in the world was he taking Wanda and not me?! And as quickly as it took me to think that and then look back at Wanda with her lipstick, even my twelve year old brain could figure out the answer to that. My jealousy and anger started to wane a bit, though my lust for the bike increased, as did the feeling I was getting from being around Wanda. Like the feeling I got from being around Sandy, only more intense.

"Yeah, that rodeo is a good time," I said. "The parade is swell. And they've got an A&W up there, too! It's a swell day for a ride!"

I didn't hear Scorchy, but I noticed Wanda's eyes shifting focus to something behind me. "Hey, Kid!" he called out, "The pan sounds pretty good."

"Hi ya,' Scorchy! Yeah it sure does. Wanda says you're headin' to the rodeo."

Scorchy went around to the front of the bike and twisted the throttle. The bike's twin pipes roared. "Yeah," he said. "Wanda wants to show me some of the country...get me out of town." He grinned at Wanda as their gazes met.

"Kid, what time are you supposed to ring the church bell?" Wanda asked.

Wanda brought me face to face with Sin Number Four: Forgetting important stuff, I guess, is like sloth when it means forgetting a job. I glanced up the street at the bank clock. It read: 9:43! "Gotta go!" I yelped, "I've got two minutes — gotta run!"

Scorchy hopped onto the bike like one of those Pony Express riders on TV, just like lightning. "Hop on, Kid!" he said. "Get'cha there in a flash!" He reached back and folded down a foot peg. I climbed on. "Watch your legs on those hot exhaust pipes!" Scorchy warned. "Put your hands around my waist and hold tight!"

I threw my arms around him, my face pressed into the leather back of his jacket. I heard the mechanical *"klatch!"* of the transmission getting into first gear then the rev of the motor. We were off the curb, onto Main Street, and at the stop sign before I could whoop in delight. Two blocks to the church and another softer "klatch" as Scorchy hit second gear. Exhaust snapped out of the pipes as Scorchy throttled down as we approached the stop sign by the church. I lifted my head and watched Scorchy pull the clutch handle. A big chrome spring in a chrome cover, the "mouse trap" levered the clutch. A heavier heavy *"klatch!"* told me he'd down-shifted. His foot came off the foot-board, landing on the pavement. Another twist of the throttle and the rear of the bike spun round. The force of the turn pulled at me, but I was still locked down tight on his waist. We braked to a stop at the curb.

"Kid, ring 'er one for me!" Scorchy said. "See you tomorrow!"

I hopped off the pillion pad back over the tail-light. "You bet, Scorch! See you tomorrow!"

I bounded up the wooden front steps and through the open door. The second hand on the steeple vestibule clock reached ten as I pulled the rope down, and as it touched eleven, I started pulling the rope to swing the bell in its cradle. At ten o'clock sharp, Scorchy's ring clanged out. Fourteen clangs later I let the rope pull through to rest the bell. All of my sins felt lifted as I shot a glance towards Scorchy through the door of the church. He snapped me a salute, cracked a grin, and then hit the throttle. The panhead roared off to Wanda and the rodeo.

I noticed Sandy on the church steps. She was staring as Scorchy faded in the distance.

"Nice bike, huh?" I said.

I felt I had her full attention.

Long Day's Night —
Wanda's Story

Wanda arrived in town on the eastbound Northern Pacific. Her journey is not quite as pleasant as the vintage ad portrays.

Scorchy's bike roared all the way to the church with just a pause at the stop sign at the top of Main. Wanda had been hoping to get out of town without any attention, but there was no chance of that with the Kid clanging that church bell. Folks would start making their way to Sunday service soon.

Scorchy cracked the throttle and made sure she knew he was on his way back. Of course, that meant that the two couples walking past the stop sign at the corner knew it, too. The two men smiled and their lips moved as they waved at Scorchy when he passed by them. Wanda felt like she could read the thoughts of their wives who stared at her while she waited for Scorchy on the sidewalk under the blacksmith sign. Wanda had seen that look more than a few times since the day she'd stepped off the train in their town. The passage of a few years hadn't made it any easier to take and their attitudes — their disdain? — seemed to never be far away.

That day — the day Wanda met Helen — had been five years earlier and for those years her whole life had been Mattie's Diner, working with Helen to keep her feet on the ground and to build up a nest egg to get somewhere else one day.

Helen had left northern California with her husband, Bob, as soon as he'd gotten out of the Air Force in 1945. They'd met and been immediately swept up in a whirlwind romance that resulted in them tying the knot right before he shipped out to fight the Japs (single-handed, to hear Bob tell it).

Once he got to the Pacific, he couldn't wait to get home. Bob's folks owned farmland in Montana, and ran some cattle as well. When he got out, that's where they headed...but things had not gone well. Turned out that Bob's mom, Beulah, was decidedly *not* keen on a California gal, even if she could work the garden. You see, Beulah had already planned Bob's happy ending, and Helen was the witch that ruined that fairy tale. That Bob had not mentioned the little fact that he was already hitched till the happy couple stepped off the train was kick in the guts to Beulah

Helen's oil met Beulah's water, and if you smelled smoke there was a fire someplace between them. The morning after their arrival, Helen walked into town and went apartment hunting. No small task, but by noon she'd landed a place. That night during an otherwise silent dinner, she announced she had found a place in town and they'd be going "home" after dinner. The ice never thawed between Beulah and Helen. The kids were in love and loyal to each other. Helen had out-waited Tojo and was damned if she'd give in to her mother-in-law Hitler.

Bob and his brothers worked on the place for his dad, but he could see the writing on the wall and decided to go back into doing the only thing he knew how to do besides farm, and that was *fly*. By 1950, Korea got him back in the military and overseas again. Helen, deciding to be practical, agreed to hold on in town till he got back stateside and then head to wherever the Air Force stationed Bob. The apartment was cheap and she'd taken a job at a local diner owned by a woman name Mattie, who was also her landlord. The two had gotten chummy and Helen eventually learned that Beulah was not the toast of the town she thought she was. Mattie had set her straight on that fact. It was a small town and it didn't take long to get in the trenches of the ladies' home front.

Bob went missing in action early on in the conflict. Helen held onto the Air Force's POW story till the boys finally came home without him. Mattie's shoulder, work, and boxes of Kleenex got them through that. And then, in 1957, Helen was laid low again when Mattie died in a car crash. A drunk on his way to Rockvale collided with her as she was driving home from Billings. To Helen's surprise, Mattie's will left everything to her. Mattie was laid to rest in the old town cemetery and Helen rolled up her sleeves and took on the diner on her own. She made work her new favorite thing, and the place ended up being popular with locals and truckers heading to and from Wyoming.

Beulah, of course, blamed Helen for Bob's death. If not for "that harlot," her boy would have been at home, not dead in some Asian prison. She did her best to poison the town against her, but Helen put her head down and did what she did best. Work hard and do right by folks.

Helen's charity began at home with those were having a hard time but were missed by the "do-good elite" or the church. People from the wrong side of small town society, tattered bums, old spinsters. Helen would show her face at mass at the little Catholic Church on Christmas Eve and Easter Morning. "Touchin' base," she called it. The rest of her religion she worked out in elbow grease and food. By 1961 she was the go-to woman for all "non-lady" issues in the community. She had friends of both genders who would "get involved" if need be with folks not acting right with their families. She had the respect and trust of the local sheriff who knew if he knocked on her door he could get a hot something for a down and out on his way to someplace else. That was Wanda's connection.

The town's train station in the mid-1900's, much the way it looked when Wanda stepped off the train. It looks much the same today.

Wanda had bummed an extra two hundred miles out of the Burlington Northern Conductor, but by three in the afternoon she knew it was the end of the line. The conductor had seen his share of girls like her, down on their luck and on the run from something. When the train pulled into town he made it clear that this was her last whistle stop on his train. He took Wanda's bag and walked it, with her attached, up to the station master. He informed him this was her stop and that she hadn't had a bite to eat since she'd boarded his train and that he'd appreciate the favor of keeping her *off* his train. The conductor didn't think she'd see the buck change hands in the shake.

Errol was the station master — and, it turned out, just about everything else part-time in town — and one of his jobs was freight delivery. He ushered Wanda into his Rambler wagon. Yeah, she knew...never go with strangers, but she'd seen some strange ones and Errol was not a problem. Wanda could read men and he read straight.

Errol hauled mail bags like this to the train and back in in his Rambler wagon. He was on a mail run when he met Wanda and took her to Mattie's.

The Rambler bumped across the tracks to the stop sign on the highway then up Main Street until he pulled up in front of a place with a sign that read "Mattie's Diner." He got out of the car, opened the back and took out a couple of boxes, and then came around to her side of the wagon. "Come on in," he said with a wag of his head. "Bring your bag."

The place had a counter, some tables, and a homemade smell that instantly switched Wanda's stomach into growl mode and started her mouth to watering like Red Riding Hood when she saw the wolf or something like that. Errol gently guided her to a stool. Leaning against the counter, he put down the buck, added a second to it, and started chatting with the woman in the apron. After a second she gave Wanda a look that released a load of bricks off her shoulders, a look that told her that it was going to be alright, maybe for just a day or maybe only an hour, but it was going to be alright.

A steaming bowl of chicken noodle soup appeared. The noodles were a half inch wide and uneven in shape, obviously homemade. A tall glass of milk landed next to it. "Take it easy, honey," said the woman in the apron. "No rush and there's plenty."

Errol had gone. There was a dull hum of conversation, clinks of flatware on service, and the ring of the register as the woman running the place took in the fruit of her labor. The afternoon customers began to thin out and as Wanda scraped the last trace of chicken broth from her bowl she began to give the place a look over. Nothing fancy, but homey...the kind of place guys on the road like to come to when they're missing home or good food or both.

The woman came back around and said, "Eastbound bus comes through about four in the morning. You can catch it right down by Muller's bar. How about a bit more soup?"

Wanda was quick with the yes to the more figuring she'd eat till the buck stopped. It was going to be a long night no matter how she cut it. No bus fare, so she'd ride her thumb to Billings and start looking for a job. Some fellas like to take advantage of a gal who is hungry. At least she'd be one up there.

The empty bowl came back steaming full.

"My name's Helen," the woman said. "I own this place. I was just about to put this in the window." She showed Wanda a hand printed sign that read, "Help Wanted, Start Now."

"The dishwasher kid quit today for a job on a ranch. I'm about out of clean dishes and this place will fill up for dinner."

"I'm Wanda." She stuck out her hand. "I'll clean up this bowl and head back to the kitchen. I'll take the job." That's how it had been, five years ago. She had landed in town, on her feet as it turned out.

The dishwasher job ended up with the two of the gals becoming a team. Wanda started working the front, too, which freed up Helen to cook and chat. When they closed that night Helen took Wanda to her place, putting her up in the spare room until she could get a place of her own. Wanda's own place never came about. She stayed in the extra room at Helen's and started feeding the payment kitty. Helen and Wanda became fast friends, and business partners. A couple of gals with pasts, dropped into a small Montana town, working for a better day tomorrow.

It's not a new story. They worked hard, got another kid to wash dishes, put up some catchy road signs, and filled the joint breakfast, lunch and dinner. They even banked some of the extra money made during the summer tourist season when they started seeing some of the same faces return the following season. The trucker trade was steady and the railroad gangs came in on paydays before they hit the bar and then headed back to their "Crummies" on the side rail, to sleep.

Some of the boys were rough around the edges, but shaped up when they came into Mattie's. Helen and Wanda both knew how to talk to men; becoming sort of a "mom n' sis" team. It only took a hint or two to quiet someone down, or his buddies educated him. The gals ran what sailors call a tight ship, never losing regular town customers to any roughhousing.

A letter arrived via general delivery to the town post office from the attorney representing the estate of Helen's step-father. One of his final acts was to direct his attorney to find Helen, tell her he was sorry for all he'd done, and that he was leaving everything to her. Following up on military records and the war time marriage license, he'd taken a shot at Helen being where Bob was from.

The letter also brought the bad news that Helen's mom was seriously ill. Helen was the only living relative left when her step-father died. From Helen's few comments as she read the letter Wanda could tell there was no love lost between her and her step-father. That could well have explained why she'd never spoken of her family; but then Wanda had never brought up her side of that issue either. Helen called and set up an emergency appointment with John Clark, the local lawyer, put a "back in an hour" sign in the window, and marched Wanda up the street.

Helen had Clark draw up papers putting the house and diner in Wanda's name until she either came back to town or sent word to do otherwise. Their next stop was the bank where she transferred the business account to Wanda. Walking back up to the diner, Helen told Wanda that the place had been a gift to her from Mattie and now she was giving it to her; to build it her way, and never look back. Helen then told Wanda she was going home to pack and was catching the afternoon train; she'd come by the diner on the way from the house to the station and that Wanda better get cracking for the dinner rush as nothing was stated.

By 4:30 the diner was full. Helen and Wanda had been a tag team for years so doing the solo thing was pushing it. Wanda fended off the "Where's Helen at?" questions and was relieved when she heard one of the men say, "Hi there, Helen, where ya been?" The volume of the hub-bub around that question ratcheted up, Helen made a gesture for everyone to quiet down.

"Friends, I have had a great eighteen years here," Helen said. "I need to go to my mother's side, but don't worry, I'm fine. Wanda is going to take care of Mattie's now. I couldn't have asked for a better gal to come along and I know you'll treat her right, just like you treated me."

We all walked her across the highway, over that tracks to the station. By the time the train rolled in it seemed half the town was there to see her off. Helen had taken to saying she'd be back when she got stuff taken care of. Friends like to hear that. In her heart Wanda knew that would be a long way off...if ever.

"Hop on, watch your leg on the pipes," Scorchy instructed. "Hold on to me...lean the same way I do."

Wanda pulled her sunglasses down over her eyes and tossed a leg over the back fender. If the

Kid could do it so could she. There was a mechanical *"klatch"* and the bike made a little shutter.

"Ok, here we go!"

And man, away they went. Wanda had never been on anything that moved that quickly in her life. Scorchy only throttled back a bit, checking left down the highway, and then opened the throttle. Wanda held on tighter as acceleration tried to pull her off the back of the bike. The pulse of the motor moved through her body and then felt weightless until a momentary cut of the throttle allowed her to settle forward against Scorchy. There was the *klatch* of a gear change and the rocket effect took off again! Zero to 65 in just a few seconds! The bike motor settled into a loud purr. Wind pulled around Wanda as she let out a squeal of excitement.

"Like that?" Scorch yelled back.

"Oh, Yessss!" she laughed, as the wind stole her words.

The '53 rolled down Montana 72 until they caught the road to Red Lodge where Scorchy swooped the bike through some turns up past the old mine. Bike riding isn't like being in a car. On the bike riders are outside, involved in nature, not insulated and traveling through it. Talk doesn't easily overcome the roar of wind and pipes. It is a time for looking outward and inward. By the time they reached Red Lodge and the rodeo all Wanda wanted was more detachment from her reality. Pulling into town the bike rolled to a stop at the 212 junction. The bike dropped into its patient idle, waiting for Scorchy.

A highway department sign read "Cooke City 69 miles." Another sign, painted on a board, read "Rodeo" with a big red arrow pointed the other way. Some poem Wanda had read in high school, one with a line about the road less traveled, crossed her mind.

Scorchy had his right foot planted on the roadbed, his head turned to Wanda. "Bike's runnin' great!" He said. He had a happy-as-hell look in his eyes.

Wanda had seen so many of the opposite kind of look in her life, she heard herself say, "I hear Cooke City is a nice drive. Steep, with a lotta' curves. But it's your rodeo, honey."

A vintage post card of the Cooke City Highway. The '53 climbed to Cooke City, the gate of Yellowstone National Park at just under 11,000 feet.

The ride to Cooke City turned out to be just

under 70 miles of steep zigzags and switch backs along the border of Wyoming toppin' out at just under 11,000 feet. Mountain crags, crystal lakes, rushing streams swollen with run-off from snow melt, and a blaze of Montana wildflowers...the bike pulled strong out of the corners, one after the other, and only got into 4th gear on the occasional longer straight shots. From the start to the Beartooth Pass they gained 5,000 feet in elevation. Every turn was a new spectacular vista of untouched wilderness. At least it seemed so, even though they were riding on a road that had been built in the nineteen-thirties. The '53 wove in and out and up and up, wind in the rider's faces, blue sky above, Wanda was climbing away from her reality. They reached a plateau and could see Pilot Peak, which looked like a tall church steeple in the distance.

Pilot Peak is visible in the center of this period post card.

Cooke City had one gas station. As Scorchy popped out the kick stand, Wanda swung her leg off the seat. It was a stretch she was glad to make. Stiff, she worked to control her numbed behind as she walked to the ladies room. Climbing away from reality is tough on a girl's rear. Scorchy had been pretty clear the '53 was set up to be ridden solo, and the best he could do was put on a racing pillion pad that would not be real comfortable after a mile or two. He was right, but Wanda wouldn't say a word about it.

Post World War II Cooke City was not much different in the mid 1960s.

Wanda came out of the station to see the '53 surrounded by a group of boys and young men, all talking at once. Scorchy had just filled the tanks and handed the kid working the pump a buck. Across the highway was a bar, Wanda caught the unmistakable smell of a hot grill and burgers.

"How about a beer and a burger?" she called to Scorchy. "Who knows...I might learn something. It's been a while since I ate anything I didn't cook! How about I walk on over and grab a stool for us?"

Scorchy snapped her a smile and salute as the gas pump kid was handing back his change. The kid perked up with a big smile. Wanda knew Scorchy had said something funny. He had a special way about him...how he looked at you, how he took the time to connect and make you feel that whatever you had done was the best he'd ever seen. At least it sure felt that way.

As Wanda walked up the steps into the bar she heard the Panhead motor catch as Scorchy kicked it into life. Inside the bar Wanda's eyes began to adjust to the dim light. There was the smell of cigarette smoke, beer, and burgers on grill.

"Hi, there doll, what can I get for ya'?" asked the barkeep.

"How 'bout a burger? Some fries and beer?"

"You bet, doll! Hey, Joey! Burger and fries!"

"Great, double it!"

"Say, doll, you gotta' watch that..."

At that moment, Scorchy walked through the door, pushing his sunglasses up over his forehead.

"Make that two, Joey!"

Lunch was okay, though Joey needed some pointers. Wanda and Scorchy bellied up to the bar, ate the burgers, nibbled the fries, and sipped the beer. The talk was small. Wanda thought she'd like it to be bigger, but wasn't that sure she'd like it when it got there.

"Hope ya didn't learn anything from Joey," Scorchy said as they left. "I like your burger and fries the way you do 'em now!" Scorchy kicked the bike through and it roared into life. It always seemed ready. Scorchy made a lot of stuff feel ready. "Hop on, Wanda," he smiled. "The road calls!"

You Wouldn't Be So Tough

I felt my lip slide around my front teeth, held in place by the force of Rick's fist. I could feel the inside of my mouth tear on the impact, taste the metallic flavor of blood erupting. In time, I would learn that you don't stop to consider these things when punches are being thrown. The brain needs to focus on either not getting hit...or hitting back.

What can you say about how it was when you

were a kid? Yeah, I did it all right, all the time, every time. Yeah, right, that rock'll float.

I grew up in a pretty secure environment. My dad was gone a lot. Him being a Navy officer, that went with the territory; but Mom ran a tight ship and with two younger sisters it was not a really rough and tumble lifestyle. Never really good at sports, I got more into model building and reading. But I had an attitude. Probably all boys have one of some kind or another. I had a dark side that would manifest in behavior that often led to trouble. Additionally — and problematically — I wasn't chicken. Once stuff started I could be counted on to show up...for better, or usually, for worse.

Horseplay, fooling around, bullying, just being a dip...call it what you want. There had been a lot of it at school. The clever trick of getting the chump to look. "See my thumb?" then a *smack* to the head with the other hand. "Gee, you're dumb! *Harharhar!*" Or the classic "center-dump" during flag football (and you're always the center). Like Lucy and Charlie Brown, you always believe next time it will be okay. Then there was "clipping," where you kicked the other guy's foot so it went behind his opposite leg and made him stumble or trip. It's a cheap shot, and just the shot needed while walking in the hallway or on the stairs with desired result being that they crash into the person in front of them — a girl, hopefully — so that she drops her books and everyone turns and says, "*Gawd!* What a klutz!"

Having been victim of the "clip" on a number of occasions, I had pretty well mastered the technique and decided to try it out. The bell rang and we were off to the gym, which took us down the stairs. Rick was my best target of opportunity. He wasn't an upper class kid. In my estimation he was more of a peer. In retrospect, I should have picked someone else. Better to take on someone who thinks they are better than you. Always fight *up*. But being the new kid in town, I hadn't yet figured out where I really was in the social structure and fell prey to the lure of behaving like one of the elites...and picking on others is what they did.

On the second to the last step, I was in perfect sync, my right leg coming forward when Rick's left was back. At the precise moment I swung my foot in a precisely aimed arc.

Tap!

Rick stumbled forward. There was no girl or boy to land on, so he fell straight to the ground, on his knee. It wasn't possible to tell if he was hurt. The banter started. The hoots, the laughs. You make choices all your life and a lot of right ones end up being made because you made some wrong ones first.

"You tripped me!"

There was pain and embarrassment in his face and eyes. I could have said, "Man, I was clumsy!" or "I didn't mean to!" or simply, "I'm sorry!" but I made the wrong choice. I looked at him, joined in with everyone else, and said, "Man, you're a klutz!"

Time passed and Rick's knee became a problem for him. In those days kids sucked it up or got over it, but eventually he had to wear a brace and he stopped talking to me. I heard about it over and over from other kids. Embarrassed, I denied all — I hadn't done it — and reinforced my story until lying and pride had me trapped in a corner.

Weeks passed and the event started to fade into memory as summer approached, but there were stirrings in the kid undercurrent. Those eager to see conflict between people other than themselves were slowly toiling away and spreading discord. One day at lunch I was informed that Rick would finally dispense his punishment for my treacherous act in the park after school.

The school day ended and as the school emptied, both of us were swept up in the student swell towards the park. Both of us had a dedicated corps ranting on about how each of us was going to pound the other. A couple of smart kids would have seen that they were becoming the circus of the day, the entertainment, and would have looked around and said, "Screw this." Smart kids would have said something to get the problem sorted out. They would have said, "Let's do this alone later." But kids aren't smart. The only upside was that our clash would be restricted to fists and that it was understood nobody would get stomped. This was about honor.

Neither of us were brawlers. At the park we indulged in some weak posturing before the crush pushed us together. His fist found my lip. I punched him back in the ribs. He drew blood but didn't want more. We backed off from each other and it was done, a real disappointment to the crowd. I never did apologize and that was wrong. On a one to ten scale of questionable things I've done it was a one, or a two. There was no honor.

After that, the school year finally wound down to its end. It was 1965 and I was twelve and in just a few weeks events and a 1953 Harley Davidson would bring me together with Scorchy Black.

Summer was passing too fast. Having a "job" did that to time, and I spent every minute I could at "work."

Wednesday was no different than any other day. I'd taken care of my chores at home and I didn't have a lawn to mow that day, so after a bowl of Post cornflakes with freeze-dried blue berries and a glass of Tang (the official drink of NASA and the astronauts), I was out the door. Fritz the dog fell in with me, but he couldn't go to the shop. I turned towards him, spread my legs, and planted my feet, doing my best imitation of my dad. "Fritz!" I called out, "You stay home!"

Fritz's butt immediately hit the ground in the

yard. Dejected, he'd watch until I was out of sight and then head to the back steps to lie around waiting for something else interesting.

As I crossed the street by the park, I noticed a group of kids hanging out around a picnic table. Not usually seen in town, they were the local "gentry's" kids. They really seemed to have it going for them. Motivated by what was important in a small town — being a jock or a cheerleader — a kid's social standing and success was backed by what his folks, their folks, and then their folks did on their land, who they'd bought out, their new tractors and trucks, and so on. When I'd first got to town, I'd operated under the illusion that if I was friendly and made an effort, I would quickly make some friends. I'd been wrong. I had tried sports. No great shakes, so there was no reason to bother with me as far as the social order went.

I noticed that the group was pretty much made up of the same kids who pushed for my fight with Rick, which had been little more than an afternoon's amusement for them. "Hey, queer!" one of them shouted at me.

Adrenalin started to rise. Fight or flight became the question. To react or not to react. They hadn't moved off the far away picnic table. I was now half way through the park.

"Where you goin'? Come'ere!"

At the railroad crossing, the light began to flash red and the bell rang as the striped cross arm barriers descended across the road in front of the rails. *Right on time. The south bound freight to Wyoming.* By the time I was at the park's far edge the boys were off the table, bunched together and coming my way. Ignoring them was rousing their anger. To them, my silence was dismissive, insulting.

"Hey, queer, I said come'ere!"

The roar of the diesel and the clack of the steel wheels on rails made a loud, steady beat. The engine was at the far station marker.

Not today boys, I thought.

I turned towards the park. Making sure I had their attention, I gave them a one-finger salute. It was a flagrant violation of class and the gang sprinted towards me. But suicide was not my plan. My strategy, based on solid knowledge of my environment, was calculated in a flash of neurons:

One, the train always traveled at the same speed.

Two, while the train looked gigantic, it was really only big length-wise and only a few yards wide.

Three, the engineer would blow the horn like crazy if he thought someone wasn't paying attention. There was no way he could stop, and that really was scary.

Four, it would take me just a few seconds to cross the tracks from a dead stop.

Five, once across I would only have to deal with the highway and then I'd be at the shop. Once I reached the shop (and Scorchy) I would be safe.

Six, the only real problem was finding the courage (more like lack of it) to overcome that little voice in my head, the one that always says, "you can't do this!" in the middle of doing it.

"Yer dead, queer!"

They were close enough to hear over the train and the crossing bell. I side-stepped in front of the crossing post and threw another salute. The engineer started to lay on the air-horn when he saw I wasn't keeping a safe distance from the crossing.

Whaaaaa Whaaaaa Whaaaaaaaaaaaaa!

The ground shook as the engine started to cross in front of the station. The gang broke past the edge of the park, crossing the road now. I couldn't help leaping into the air and waving *"come on!"*

WHAAAAA!! W H H A A A A A A A !!! W W W W H H H A A A A A A A A !!!!

They were close enough for me to see the whites of their eyes. Now was the time to turn...*and RUN!!!!!*

I can only imagine what the engineer was screaming as he pulled the air-horn off its ceiling mount. I was totally focused on ignoring the screaming voice in my head telling me to stop, but to stop now, on the tracks, would mean death by train! I tore over the crossing, the engine close enough to touch, and cleared the tracks to reach the far side. A head with a railroad cap over a pale face jammed itself out the engine's side window on a neck that seems to stretch out a couple of feet. The conductor's mouth turned from the "O" of terror to the "U" of a smile before flipping into a frown.

On the other side of the rumbling train, the boys at the back of the pack slammed like dominoes into the back-peddlers up front who did the sensible thing: slammed to a stop against the crossing guard-rail.

Pursuit was impossible. My timing had been perfect. I paused and turned a few yards from the tracks as the engine and the first freight cars rolled by. The train would take as long as fifteen minutes maybe to pass through. When the first empty flat car passed, our eyes met over the rolling steel. Adrenaline still pulsed in my veins. I had faced both a pounding and probable death only seconds apart. I outwitted the former and just cheated the latter. I didn't bother to suppress a smile as I turn and ran across the highway and up Main Street past Muller's Bar.

I was starting to come down when I walked through the shop door. "Hey! Let's get to work around here!" I yelled.

Scorchy, was pulling a piece of stock steel onto the work bench. His bemused expression seemed to say, "You talkin' to me?" Scorchy lived in the back of the shop, so he had probably been working for over an hour. His expression changed to a quip of a smile.

"Hey, Kid! Nice of you to come by, grab yer gloves off the bench and help me get this in place."

I was there in a flash, pep in my step, gloves on, and I felt exceptionally strong as I lifted my end of the stock onto the metal table top. The stock was clean and smooth compared to the marred and burned work table surface. Soon, heat, molecular reaction, abrasion, and force applied by Scorchy would shape it into a replacement part for an old piece of farm equipment. Possibly even something for the father or grandfather of one of my pursuers. I basked in a glow of irony.

"Kid, roll the cutting rig over and get her fired up."

I made sure the hoses and torch were securely coiled on the tops of the green and yellow tanks and then carefully tipped the mount back and rolled it over to the table. Uncoiling the hose, I closed the two control knobs on the torch before setting it on the table. Returning to the tanks, I opened both brass valves to start the flow of gas to the torch. Picking up the torch and cracking the control knobs, I could hear the hiss of the gas mix as it streamed out the nozzle. Next came the hard part, getting the striker flint to spark and ignite the stream of gas. Scorchy always made it look easy, but sometimes I couldn't get a spark and I was sure the gas build up would explode...but I kept at it until I got it. Keeping at it was Scorch's way of teaching. First he'd show you, then he'd have you do it, then if you didn't do it right he'd have you do it again. When you got it right he'd have you do it as often as possible to keep the lesson in your head.

The shops gas rig cart.

The second snap of the striker handle got a bright spark and there was a dull pop followed by the low roaring hiss of the burning gas. The black sooty smoke cleared, wafting away to become part of the story of years of jobs encrusted on the shop's ceiling and walls. I dialed in the knobs to get a blue–white flame. Scorchy took the torch from my hand.

"Goggles."

He'd already put his in place and waited until I did the same before starting the cut. Heated pieces of metal cascaded onto the bench and danced on the floor, blasted free by compressed gas, only to disappear, becoming part of the iron dust that lingered in the shop corners.

When the new shapes were released from the hold of the stock and then joined into a new form by arc of the welder, I was put to work with a grinder to smooth the rough cut and welded edges with clear instructions to "Clean up just the big stuff" while Scorchy got to work on the drill press.

Scorchy had finished the work on the press and then fitted the bolts. "Hey, Kid!" he said, "Feel like lunch to you?" Lunch for Scorchy was across the street at Mattie's Diner which was really Wanda's. For me it was back home, which was past the park, down River Road and then back. "Go toss the bolt on the back door while I shut down this stuff."

When I pushed the back door closed I caught

a glimpse of a couple of the boys in the alley. A dark and bloody scenario played out in my head as I shuffled up to the front where Scorchy was waiting. We walked out the front door. As Scorchy turned to lock it up, I noticed that both ends of the street were blocked. Maybe it was the boys coming from around back, coming into view down in Miller's parking lot or maybe it was the look on my face, but something tipped Scorchy off. "Looks like somebody is looking for trouble," he said as he turned. "Know anything about it?"

"Yeah, I know about it."

"Gonna be able to handle it?"

"Depends if you mean how well I take a beatin' means how well I handle it? I had the nine o'clock south bound to get me out of it this morning."

"That sounds interesting, let's talk about that at Wanda's."

Scorchy stepped off the curb and I followed, across Main Street, over the little ditch that ran next to the sidewalk, and into the diner.

Flatware rattled on dishes, half a dozen conversations, kitchen sounds, plus the smells that always filled Mattie's. Then there was Wanda. Wanda was no kid, but not old either. I'd seen her in two outfits, the usual waitress outfit she wore in the diner and once in some jeans and leather coat. Both fit snug and something about how she looked made me warm. I'd heard some of the older boys talk about her, how she was a "looker" and "divorced." Wanda always had a smile for Scorchy, even more so since they took that ride to the rodeo on the '53.

We popped — well Scorchy popped, I kinda slumped — onto the counter stools. "Hey, Doll," Scorchy called out. "What's the special?"

"Doll?" that was new for Scorchy.

"Chicken fried steak, mashed potatoes, drippings gravy, and garden peas," Wanda replied.

She and Scorchy looked at each other for a while. I think she was tryin' to suck his brain out or something when somebody, not me, coughed.

"Hey, what about you, Kid?" she asked. "You look like a condemned man. What ya want for your last meal?"

"Kid's got a problem we gotta talk about," Scorchy said. "How 'bout given him a special. OK, Kid?"

I sipped on my milk and Scorchy drank his coffee until Wanda set our plates down. I spilled my guts about the morning. Scorchy perked right up when I told him the rail road crossing part.

Wanda stood behind the lunch counter. She made a little glance left and right like she was checking to see if anyone was looking or listening and then made a little flip of her head which caused the red pony tail in the back to flip. She leaned down in front of me, putting her elbows on the counter, and I found myself staring right at her cleavage.

"Kid," I heard through a hormonal fog.

"Kid!"

A waitress leans in on the counter, unfortunately there is no photo of Wanda from this time, but she got Kid's attention.

I came out of it looking into her green eyes. They were framed above and below with thick lashes that floated when she blinked. She had slight shadow, a green shade, just below her dark red eyebrows. The eyes seemed to be looking into my soul.

"Look, Kid," Wanda said. Her full red lips moved in the shapes that made words and I began to hear her low, quiet, but firm voice. "If the problem is some of those boys outside, they're what their folk either made 'em or let 'em become. I know a couple of them from here, comin' in with their folks. Some think that they own a bit more than what they have a deed to. World's full of folks like that and they'll push ya and take ya for all they can. Time comes you gotta stand, can't run. You may not win, but you don't make it easy." I think my mouth was hanging open a bit as she straightened up and went to freshen up coffees.

Scorch nudged me in the ribs. He had a funny grin on his face. "Nuff said, I think. Eat."

"Get the blanket off the bike," Scorchy said. "Push it out back and get it warmed up. We need to go some place private for an hour or two."

I stood there trying to process the sensory overload of the last hour. First Wanda and now get the bike out!

"Kid, get to it! I'm puttin' the closed sign in the window. Back in a couple of hours."

I pulled the blanket off the Harley Davidson. As usual the chromed pieces and the flaming paint job caught my eye.

Focus!

The panhead was heavy but low to the ground and the back door was level onto the gravel. I unscrewed the gas shutoff valve, reached down and moved the choke lever into the closed position, then opened the throttle. Climbing on the footboard I pushed the kick peddle through till I felt the compression take hold and then pushed it through, twice. Switching the choke to half open and turning the dash switch on, I put all my weight on the kick peddle and got ready to push down when I remember to reach down and retard the spark. Now safe from getting kicked back, I laid all my weight into the downward kick. The bike caught and roared into life. I quickly twisted the throttle back down, moved the spark advance into the run position, and the bike started to idle.

Potato, potato, potato...

"Looks like you got the knack of that. Put this on your head so I don't catch hell for what I'm about to do." Scorchy popped the old helmet that had been in the boxcar at home. "Just put it on, your dad left it here." Scorchy mounted the bike and opened the choke up. I climbed onto the back of the bike. "Kid," he said, "I'm gonna idle easy n' slow down the alley. Just sit up straight like this is your bike. When we get to the highway I'll tell you when to hang on...then *hang on.*"

I sat up straight and tall. I followed Scorchy's gaze to Muller's gravel parking lot where the boys were still waiting for me. We paused for a moment at the edge of the highway, pointed south. "Hang on!" He said. I did and we took off, gravel flying. Scorchy took the '53 all the way into forth gear. We were flying.

A few miles down the highway was the turn-off to the dump. That's where we ended up. Scorchy parked the bike, unfortunately upwind of the smoldering garbage piles, and told me to get off. He swung his leg over the bike and took off his leather coat before he spoke. "Kid, there ain't no easy way to do this in a couple of hours, but I'm gonna show ya how to maybe not get your ass kicked too bad this afternoon. By the time we're done you'll know somethin' about fightin' and that helps with confidence."

I really wasn't sure what to expect, I was scared, out here by myself. *Going to fight.* I thought about what Wanda had said. I thought about Wanda.

"Put your glasses on the bike seat," Scorchy said. "You won't be wearing those. First things first. You gotta stand up to 'em when they come at you, and to do that you gotta be able to stand strong."

The two hours went by in seconds. I learned how to stand, to wait, to block, to get out of some basic holds and how to hit with not just a fist but some variations. Scorch threw punches for me to block, some blocks I missed and even his "pulled" training punches stung. My nose got tagged, bled a bit, and I was sure I had a bruise or two. He let me hit him. It felt like hitting a tree. He encouraged me to hit harder. Finally saying, "They should feel that." We worked "combinations" and finished up with a lecture.

"These guys just want to push you around and probably don't want or really know how to fight. Pick the mouthiest one and focus on him. If you stand up, break a few grabs, block a punch he may well be done with it. You're no fun and a hard target. If he comes at you, work the blocks and work in with the combination and hit him. If it hurts he's gonna watch himself. If ya hit him and he goes down, let him be. Just watch him and let him get up and go or let him try again. There's a time and place for not lettin' the other guy up, but this ain't it. If you get knocked down, get up and go again. You got nothin' to lose as those boys are bigger than you. They prove nothin' beatin' on ya, they lose everything if you beat them. Kid, you got guts, I already know that. You can handle this. Let's go and get it done."

As the panhead roared back towards town, the wind cooled the bruises on my face. It was three-thirty in the afternoon when Scorchy took a right across the tracks. The rigid frame bounced me hard on the rear pillion seat. He pulled up next to the group of boys, who had all jumped up from the park picnic table not quite sure what to make of the arrival of what they probably thought were the Huns. Scorchy gestured for me to get off the bike.

"You wouldn't be so tough without your biker friend around," One of the boys said.

Scorchy could have said something like, "I'm here to make sure it stays fair," or "That sounds tough when there's five of you and one of him," or he could have just stared 'em down, but he didn't. "Give me the helmet, Kid," was all he said. Then he gave me a wink, kicked the pan into gear, and took off, looping around and back towards town. Six heads turned and watched.

I moved a bit to my right to get off the curb and onto level ground in the park, putting a tree to one side and a big, red brick barbecue behind me. *"Cover your back!"* I heard Scorchy say in my head. I took my glasses off and laid them on top of the barbecue. *"Draw it out of 'em, let them come to you and commit."*

None of 'em moved.

"That was pretty crazy with the train this morning," LeRoy said as he took a step forward. "Bet the conductor radioed the cops. What'cha gonna say to Bentz 'bout that when he drags your butt in?"

Scorchy's voice echoing in my head had boosted my confidence a little. I'd learn about saving face later on, but just then what I needed most was to say something to either get things rolling, or over, or both. "I was havin' fun," I said. "Just like I'd tell him I'm havin' fun now."

LeRoy was still a step ahead of the others, his eyes shifted from me to them and back to me. "You slide this time, punk."

There were a few rude comments. I stood there with my confidence gradually fading as time ticked away. I heard the crunch of tires on gravel as a car passed behind me.

"You ain't worth the trouble." LeRoy turned and walked away. The others followed.

It was like Scorchy had said. It wasn't going to be fun anymore! I'd called their bluff! It was four o'clock in the afternoon. In seven hours I had cheated death and a beating, lusted after a woman, gone at least 100 miles an hour on a motorcycle, learned how to fight, put courage into doing the honorable thing, and said something cool.

Putting my glasses back on my face, I turned to head for home...and there was Tom, the sheriff, leaning against his patrol car.

"Son, you over that morning kind of craziness now?"

"Sheriff," I replied, "That kind of craziness won't be necessary...ever again."

Hook, Line and Sinker

Even though Nancy Sinatra's hit song came a bit later in the 60s this 45 record sleeve is a perfect example of Go-Go boots and a mini-skirt.

The Beatles, Rolling Stones, Dickeys, peg leg jeans...it was the British Invasion and it was everywhere. On the TV, in the news, magazines, and all the stores. It was miniskirts and go-go boots that distracted boys, girls, teachers, and the principal at my school when a couple of girls brought the "Mod" look to class.

Margi and Cher, a couple of local lookers, ironed their blond and black hair flat, cut their bangs just above their heavily lined eyebrows that arced above heavily shadowed eyes with l-o-o-ong dark lashes. Daily one or the other, or both, performed what became sort of a ritual: standing on a stool as the principal, Mr. Stokes, used a 12 inch ruler to check hem-to-knee distance. Margi came from a town family, and it seemed her fishnet stockings became way more familiar to Stokes. Cher came from farmer-rancher stock and both of her brothers were starters on the school ball teams, so her legs became somewhat less familiar.

Girls iron each others hair flat to fit into a fashion trend set off even in rural America by *British Mod Fashion Invasion*.

It was the fall of 1965, my first year in the high school building as a seventh grader. I had just experienced the most life-changing summer "working" for the town's newest arrival, a biker from California who had taken over old Stubby's blacksmith shop. I had also just turned thirteen years old and I felt grown up, and like every other boy in school, I looked forward to seeing both of those girls since looking was as close as any of us got as they were upper class and had senior guys.

As I look back, I have to say that what I took as catching a break wasn't. But at the moment it all started I was, as my Navy dad would say, "All ahead full!"

As I get older, I tell younger folks to learn all you can about all you can as you never know what'll come in handy. Living in Texas, every kid in public school took basic Spanish (three years worth for me). Being a white kid, I treated it like a joke; but it was a grade, so Mom and I worked at my Spanish book, often rolling in laughter making jokes of some of the words, which actually put a lot of it in my head.

Part of expanding the educational horizons of Montana kids was the "assemblies" program where schools brought in knowledge and experiences from the great outside world. That fall we were to learn about Mexican culture from a traveling dance and song troupe through the rhythmic stomp of feet, clap of hands, songs of the land, and flashes of full ruffled skirts. As I write this, it occurs to me that we ignored the Mexican migrant worker kids who came for the beet field work, like they were invisible. How much better it would have been to then integrate myself with those Mexican girls with my Spanish. I bet I would have learned a lot more than new sentence structures.

Assembly attendance was mandatory, but who was fighting getting out of class? We filed into the school theater, filling the rows in the front. Not paying much attention as a couple of the guys swapped spaces in line around me so they could sit with their pals, I turned to go down the aisle to my seat and that's when I saw those legs! My bugged-out eyes traced those legs upwards from white go-go boots to white fishnet stockings, over crossed knees, finally sloping down to thighs and a white knit mini dress and a cascade of bleached blond hair that belonged to Margi. I sat down next to her. She didn't seem to notice. She was talking to another girl and a seventh grade boy was nothing to take notice of, not worth a glance.

I sat quietly, slumped in my seat, breathing in the smell of her perfume and feeling the slight warmth radiating from her body. With introductions to the student audience coupled with threat-veiled-encouragement for good behavior, the show began. From the first number it was clear that, except for me, only the migrant kids understood the words to the songs as the troupe danced about. I found myself getting the meaning courtesy of my Texas grade school Spanish. I began to translate in a whisper to no one. Margi turned to me, and I fully expected to be told to shut up, but instead heard her whisper, "You understand the songs?"

"Si, ah, yes a bit of it, learned in Texas," I whispered back.

She leaned into me, "Tell me more of what they are saying."

And so it went through the show. At the end she grabbed my hand and brought her frosty lip gloss so close to my face I was sure I could taste it. "That was far out that you know Spanish. I wish I knew how to speak Spanish."

Later in life I would define decisive action in the words of Sir Winston Churchill: "Action this day." Later, the ancient Latin phrase "carpe diem" or "seize the day" would be made relevant again in a movie starring Robin Williams. My attempt to seize that moment was typical of my younger years — real fast and lacking forethought. The moment was pure hormones coursing through my bloodstream. "I see you in study hall 3rd period," I said. "I have a book, I can teach you to hable Espanola...to speak Spanish!"

"That would be so cool, so way out!" Margi replied. "I'll see you tomorrow in 3rd! Don't you forget!"

It was more likely that pigs would fall from the sky than I might forget. I took the bus home and skipped my ritualistic watching of 'Where the Action Is" on TV. No time for Paul Revere and the Raiders that afternoon. Instead, I dove into my boxes of stuff from Texas, dug out my Spanish workbook, and started to brush up for my first lesson with Margi.

Like a bee to a flower, I was drawn. I was giving Spanish lessons to one of the best-looking girls in the school district. I was spending an hour with her every day! I was getting a delicious ribbing from every guy in the school. I savored their jealousy.

Each night I spent hours on the next day's lesson to make sure I had the pronunciation down while I dreamt of what combination of skirt, stockings, and lip gloss she'd be wearing. Margi seemed delighted to be learning a language. I tingled at compliments and had heat flashes when she held my hand and thanked me. Rapidly my teaching career evolved into an epic romance. It was all one-sided, of course. She had the looks and the ways that let her just pass time with boys (and later with men), getting what she wanted while giving back only what she wanted in return. I was merely more fun than study hall. She had her life's course plotted with her boyfriend, John. Her life would not follow that carefully plotted course, but then whose does? But the young never know that.

In Texas learning Spanish was mandatory in the school Kid attended. Kid's mom would try to make up funny meaning to the vocabulary words so he could remember them. Kid had saved his book and dusted it off for his lessons with Margi.

There is a reason why there are jealous older "boyfriends." They are a part of nature, put in place to prevent natural selection from claiming young fools before their time. It is the natural duty of the older to scare off the younger in such a way that they will not return to the folly of love, or lust, for a season...but John was not up to the task nature had appointed for him. Focused on the football season, he didn't have the time for Margi. The dumb kid — me — teaching her Spanish might keep her busy until after basketball season, at which time he'd run me off. If only he'd been up to the task nature had given him.

Older in years, a man looks back on his journey through life and it seems amazing how much he did or did not do in such a short time. The velocity at which I reached the first climactic phase of the Margi story was rapid, three to four weeks at the most at the end of which Margi had learned some Spanish before moving on to learn typing during third period.

I was sitting at the study table we used in the library when the bell ended and Margi had not come in to take her seat next to me. About ten minutes into the period, I checked out the restroom pass and took the long way to the boys' room. As I passed the rhythmic clacking of the Olympia manual typewriters in the business and office machines classroom I snuck a peak in the door and spotted Margi struggling to master touch typing.

Man...*now* that seems so strange. Back then only a few kids learned how to type! I remember messing around and not getting an elective chosen and getting stuck with some other jokers in typing in high school. Yucks was on me when the teacher was a babe. None of the guys ever looked at the keys or the book when they typed and it turned out to be one of the most useful classes I ever took as life played through.

I went back to the library and waited for the bell then, ripped back up to the typing room. I was working on my best polite. I must have been a sight to those upper classmen, Margi and her friends, as I made my way into the crowd. My "Margi...*Margi*," registered above the hallway din and she looked at me. The look was one somebody might give a down and out or a crying baby on a plane. I felt my shoulders slump and with them my whole life fell into worthlessness.

"Reach down and grab a handful, now get over that wall soldier!" I'd hear that years later, but for now I had that feeling. I plucked up and straightened up, giving it the "ole college try!" as dad would say.

"Margi, I can stop by your place in the evening..." I started to say. I may as well had just dropped my pants and took a shit on the floor. The din stopped...you could hear the door squeak at the far restroom. Out of nowhere John's long distance pass throwing hand connected to his bale bucking arm grabbed me by the neck. His "What the Hell you sayin'?" combined perfectly with the shove that propelled me most of the way down the hall into a pile on the floor. The laughter was only exceeded by the slicing wit of the commentary. I picked up my books and went back to my own part of the school where my ridicule prove to provide the greatest source of entertainment of the last month. It was so bad that the girl everyone made fun of (why for the life of me I don't remember) came up and asked me if I was ok.

The final mental knee to the groin.

I had been a young male suffering from hormone-induced, temporary insanity where I could not register reality as I plunged headlong into disaster. The day just kept getting better! My grades had gone down the toilet while I was spending my time teaching Spanish to a senior hottie at the exclusion of all else. Not only was today the day to try and fly down Senior Hall, it was also end of the quarter and the day report cards were set to be sent home.

Back then, report cards were printed cards with your grade and comments written by your teachers with ink. I was never a stellar student, but I'd never had a D before in any subject, let alone an F. This quarter my average was in the toilet and so was my life. It was 3:20 PM on a Friday and the warrant for the end of life as I knew it would come due at about four o'clock when my mom pulled the card out of the envelope.

The best laid plans of kids often fail.

I stopped at Mattie's Diner on the way home. I needed some place to take action. A couple of truckers were finishing up their coffee and pie during the lull before the evening rush. Wanda was cleaning up the counter. She looked up when the bell rang as I opened the door.

"Hey, Wanda, can I sit for a few minutes? I need to think about stuff."

"Hey, Kid. Sure...you want somethin'?"

I felt around in my pocket. I hated to be bummin' a spot to sit without buyin' something. Scorchy had never walked into the diner without at least buyin' a cup of coffee. But my pocket was empty. "No, thank you," I said. "If you don't mind, can I just sit a minute?"

"Sure, Kid, take a load off."

I chose a chair that put me with my back to the main section of the counter. I wanted to seclude myself and I needed privacy. I needed to buy some time until I could get back on track at school. Taking out my ink eraser I began to erode my failures on the card. Then, with my own pen, I started to recalibrate my grades to match the previous quarter.

"Thought you'd like a Coke."

I started as Wanda's voice shot through me like a zillion volts! She set the Coke, with a straw stuck to the side of the frosty glass, down on a napkin on the table. I felt like my face was on fire as I looked up. She didn't say a word. She didn't frown or *tisk* or smirk. She just looked at me for a second and then went back to the counter. How much had she seen? How much did she know? I double-checked to make sure the eraser crumbs were all gone. The job looked ok. It had to be. I put the card back in the envelope.

Pulling the paper off the straw, I stuck it into the Coke. It was Wanda who had encouraged me to stand up and do the right thing with a bunch of kids earlier that summer. I was fast to make decisions, good or bad, often as not to *not* do the right thing, the honorable thing.

I'd just failed, again.

"Thanks for the Coke." My voice was flat, ashamed to even look up at her. I walked out the door and took a left down the sidewalk down Main Street to the highway. Pausing at the railroad crossing, I was hoping for a freight train, thinking maybe I should just hop one and leave town so as not to be an embarrassment. No bells clanged, no signals flashed. I walked on.

Just past the park I heard the familiar sound of Scorchy's '53 panhead, first accelerating through several gears, and then the barking of the exhausts as it idled down and pulled up next to me. Scorchy was in his work clothes. Normally he never wore the leather chaps out. I could see the smudges up to where his welding goggles rested while he cut or brazed with the torch.

"Kid, you been a stranger. Hop on. Let's go have a Coke, I'll buy, you fly!"

I hesitated a minute checking my feet.

"Get on," he said. He wasn't asking.

About thirty seconds later I was dropped off at the IGA with a couple of nickels. "I'll put the bike in the shop," Scorchy said. "You hurry up with the Cokes, I'm parched!"

When you're wrong you feel strange. When you feel strange you feel beat and tired. It was work to pull the two pops out of the machine. I realized I did not have empties to put in the yellow wooden bottle rack.

Mrs. Eddy was behind the counter nearly hidden by a scale, cash register and last minute grab item racks. "Haven't seen you in awhile," she said. "How is your grandmother?"

"She's fine." I held up the bottles. "Can I bring these back in a bit? Scorchy just dropped me off."

"Sure! Mr. Black sure spends a lot of time over at Matti's. He must like Wanda's cookin' or something,' huh?"

My mind was in another place. "Thanks," came out of my mouth and I headed out the worn wooden screen door and turned left up the street. In the shop, Scorchy was waiting in the front. I handed him his Coke. He snapped the top off on the table edge, then handed it to me. I handed him the other in return. After he snapped the top off that one, he took a drink and made the little appreciative sound he always made, like it was the best thing he'd ever had to drink. He paused as he looked at the bottle. "A little red-headed bird says we need to talk about makin' choices."

I guess it took me about ten minutes to tell Scorchy the whole story, including the forgery in progress. When I looked up his bottle was empty. So was I.

"Let me see the report card."

After I handed it over he walked back into the rear of the shop, near the work area. "Sometimes it is easier to make the right choice if ya stick with folks who want to see you do right, and not take advantage of ya. Ya got a lot to learn about life, Kid. If you could go back in time for an hour what would ya do?"

"I'd never have changed the marks on the report card, I know my folks will be mad as hell about the grades but they're gonna be furious that I tried to con 'em. Scorchy, I just need a little time to get it right. I made a mistake...well a few mistakes. I should know better about girls." Scorchy chuckled. "But I know I know better about lyin'."

"Well, girls are one thing. You got a lot of mistakes comin' there, it just comes naturally. About not lyin,' you just climbed a little higher on that ladder." Scorch held the report card over the glowing forge. "I can eliminate one of the lies, and you can just 'fess up to the failing grades. I'll call yer ma and say we were talking about the grades and I sneezed and the card fell in. I'll tell the school the same thing. They'll make a new card. Teacher's got the grades in the book. Nobody but the redhead, me, 'n you'll know about the eraser 'n pen hocus pocus."

I felt my throat swell. Scorchy was in my corner. He knew what I was facing. "No, I'm gonna just take it home and tell the folks I failed, then I failed again. But now I'm working on winning."

"Finish your Coke, Kid, 'n take the bottles back. I'll give ya a ride home."

What a Dish!

A wall hung pay phone was the way to keep in touch while on the move in the 1960s. Scorchy puts one on the shop wall to provide Ace and Anna Murphy with a way to get in touch without a listed number. Wanda has one on the wall of the diner so her trucker clients can check in with dispatch while they stop to eat. She offers Scorchy a roll of dimes to make the call to Anita's father.

The newly installed pay phone was ringing as I walked through the front door. Scorchy'd had the phone guy crank up the volume and the whole thing shook.

"Scorchy!"

The sound of the trip hammer rang from the back mingled with that of the forge fan. You could just about set off a bomb up front and Scorchy wouldn't have known it.

Scorchy said he'd put the phone in the shop's front for customers to use if they had to wait. I'd asked why a pay phone, not just a phone.

"I gotta pace myself and if I have to feed dimes it keeps the calls down. Local calls are free and you get your coin back, I just keep one in the return so you got no excuse to not tell your ma you are here."

I wondered why he wasn't in the phone book.

"Stubby never had a number in the yellow pages," he'd said. "Why change tradition?"

Since it was ringing, I grabbed the hand set.

"Hello!"

I answered the way Scorchy had instructed me. I wanted to shoot off something like "Stubby's Blacksmith! Kid speakin,' can I help you?!" But "Hello" was what the boss said to say.

"Scorchy? Is this Scorchy?" The voice was female, nice, with that lilting Spanish accent.

"No ma'am." I wanted to continue in my best Texas polite on the phone, "This is Kid."

"Hi, Kid, this is Anna Murphy. I'm an old

friend of Scorchy's. I need to talk to him, please. My husband, Ace ..."

Over Cokes I had heard the stories of Ace Murphy the hot shot aviation mechanic and motorcycle rider. The Flying Tigers, bootleggers, Howard Hughes, German Aces, Blues harpists, friend and boss to Scorchy...Ace was a legend in my mind!

"Ace Murphy! Holy cow!" I let the phone handle drop and raced through the door back into the shop work space. "Scorchy! Ace...I mean, Anna Murphy is on the phone!"

Scorchy pulled his foot off the peddle of the hammer. "What's that?!"

"Anna Murphy!" I shouted, holding a pretend phone at my ear.

"Be right there!" He started to turn down the forge while I went back to the wall phone.

"He'll be right here, ma'am!"

"Hey Kid," Scorchy said. "Would ya grab that broom and sweep off the sidewalk?" That was Scorchy's way of saying he wanted to take the call in private. "Everything alright?" Were the first words out of Scorchy's mouth as I closed the door on the way out and dust started to fly.

When things started to go south in southern California, as clubs began to violently expand their territory, Scorchy and Ace began to see the need to begin a migration. Ace was concerned about his wife and kids...and about Scorchy, whom he'd known since the day he rolled into the shop on a bicycle he'd put a motor in. The break came when an old Navy buddy of Scorchy's dad had willed his blacksmith shop to him. Stubby was on the way out and had nobody. At the time he said he'd be damned if he'd let the place fall into the hands of "certain locals." When the lawyer's letter arrived announcing Stubby's death and that the deed to the shop awaited claim, Scorchy's dad had called him.

Scorchy took what fit in his saddle bags, hugged his dad, kissed his mom then rode north east on his '53 panhead. Having set up a future on the frontier for Scorchy, Ace quietly sold his shop for cash, keeping what he thought would be a seed of parts and tools. Discreetly loading a couple of trucks, Ace, his wife Anna, and their kids hit the road. By morning they were many miles into the journey.

Ace and Anna had settled in a small central Montana town, part of a day's drive further into the heart of Montana from Scorchy's shop. With the cash they bought a small place on the edge of town with some land, water, a few old fruit trees, and a barn and out buildings. Half the barn was filled with the seed parts and tools he brought for the shop that he would open in a year or so. Anna got busy becoming a Montana farm wife and mom. It didn't take long for Ace to land a job at a local gas station. Frank, the aging owner, was looking for an all-around wrench hand with business savvy who could wrangle the whole station while he spent more time fishing the Yellowstone and Big Horn Rivers.

"Yes, all is fine, Scorchy," Anna (I found out later) told him. "We're going to take the children to visit some sights around Montana so that they feel more at home here. Frank wants a couple of weeks off for a big fishing expedition, so Ace figured this would be a good time for our family to see the sights. I wanted you not to worry if you call and get no answer."

"Hear anything from home? How's your family?"

"Scorchy...things are not so good. Dad is getting older and he is being pushed to give up being president of the club. There is so much fighting now with the gringo gangs coming down. No longer is it about racing. The clubs are now about power. Many more cops, too."

Anna paused. Scorchy heard a small sigh. "I am happy we are here. Next year I will have a garden, chickens, maybe a goat or cow. Lee wants to play basketball all the time with the boys in town and Maria wants a horse. But I think about my family. Rich says Anita is seeing too much of some of the gringo boys. Scorchy, she is just a girl, my cousin."

Anita, like Anna was light skinned, like a permanent tan, with brunette hair. Scorchy last saw her on the back of one of the guy's bikes before he left. She wasn't the kid he'd met when he came home in 1960.

"Anna, she isn't a kid anymore," Scorchy replied. "Her parents are smart and her brothers aren't to be fooled with. She'll be ok."

"I hope you are right, I haven't heard from anyone for a week or so. Okay, so we will leave in a little bit."

"Say hey to Ace 'n the kids! Have a nice time and get some pictures so I can have 'em here!"

"OK, I will do that. Bye, Scorchy."

As Scorchy hung up the phone, the loneliness of his new life hit him. He'd had his folks, Ace 'n Anna, dozens of Anna's family...and he had the club. Now...

Scorchy opened the door and leaned in the doorway. "Now I got you," he said.

I turned, pulling up the broom, "What's that, Scorchy?"

"Dusty work, Kid. Makes me thirsty. I'll buy, you fly. Make mine a Coke."

Eager to have an early morning break I parked the broom against the wall. When I took the dime out of Scorch's outstretched hand he had a sad look which was something I hadn't seen before.

That afternoon's east bound bus stopped in the parking lot of Muller's bar with a loud whoosh of air from the brakes. Then, with a roar of the pusher diesel, it pulled back out onto the highway to continue its journey to Laurel and then Billings and beyond.

Greyhound Lines was, and still is, the major transcontinental bus line service in the country. Busses like this General Motors PD-4104 with revolutionary aluminum body crisscrossed the nation before the rise of air travel. They connected almost every small town in the nation. A bus like this brings Maria to town.

She stood there in a bright red dress, white shoes, matching bag. Her suitcase didn't match. It had been on the road before. Bright red lipstick accented a smile. Half a dozen heads turned as she walked into the bar.

Once inside, she inquired, "Excuse me please, can one of you gentlemen tell me where I might find Mister Black?"

Ole Harlsonn got up from his bar stool. "You mean the smith?"

"Not Smith…Black. He fixes motorcycles."

"Yep, you mean Scorchy alright."

"Scorchy Black, yes! That is him. I have come from California to see him. Where can I find him?"

"Come to him from *Califورnnieyea,* ya say? Well, good lookin', his shop is just up the street, can't miss it. The sign says 'Blacksmith.'"

The bar room lit up as she flashed her smile. The dress was snug and when she bent to pick up her case and leave she crooned, "Oh, thank you, sir!" over her shoulder. Cartoon eyes would have popped out and followed that walk out the door and down the sidewalk.

The beers of choice at Muller's Bar, Hamm's and Olympia. Ellen would use one of these "church-keys" at the bar to either pop the top off a tall neck bottle or cut two holes in the top of a beer can.

"I'm gettin' me one of them motorsickles," Ole said with a lingering leer.

"Ole, there's more to Black than the motorcycle," the bartender, Ellen, said from behind the bar. "You old dogs have had your day. Ole, close your mouth. Who wants another beer?" That brought everyone back to reality with a beer-soaked thud. Swiggin' on the next round helped take them back to another, younger time.

The shop was locked. There was no answer to her knock. The bus ride had been long and she needed to freshen up. Spotting Mattie's Diner across Main Street, she girl made her way over.

Wanda looked up when the door bell chimed as the young girl came in. "Afternoon," she said, and with a discreet nod of her head, Wanda pointed the girl to the restroom. The noise in the diner dropped down a notch from the truckers who noticed the flash of red. They stopped eating, pie balancing precariously on forks, to stare. After a few comments and a chuckle or two, their focus returned to trucks and the road.

Returning from the bathroom, the girl walked over to Wanda. "Hi," she said. "I'm looking for Mister Black, the smith. His shop door is locked."

She was one good lookin' gal. Wanda made a quick assessment, as did the not-so-discreet truckers. What was she 16...17 going on 25?

Scorchy, what are you getting into?

Wanda had been "owned" before and while she liked Scorchy, a lot, they were friends...so she pushed the jealous little black thought back behind its little door and tried to lock it. "He is probably out making a delivery. Why don't you sit down here at the counter? Coffee?"

Wanda's back was to the door as she went for the coffee urn when she heard the door bell. She glanced over her shoulder to see Ole shuffling towards the counter. After setting a full cup in front of the girl, Wanda went to check on the truckers and then saddled up across the counter from Ole. "Been over to Muller's?"

"How'd ye guess that?"

"Shot in the dark. Need a cup of Joe before you head home?"

"I sure could, and maybe a slice of your pie. That'd sure go down good!" Ole turned his attention up the counter. "Well, hey there, young missy from *Californnieyea!* You find Scorchy yet?" He turned to Wanda, with a wink, "Said she came to him all the way from *Californnieyea!*"

The little black thought was pushing out of its little door again. "That's a long way to come all the way to this little town. Have you known Scorchy for long?"

"Oh, yes!" she replied. "Since I was a girl! I was always at the shop! He took me for rides on the bikes he worked on! My cousin Anna, she says Scorchy he's a good man...that a girl would do well with a man like Scorchy Black."

When he arrived at the diner, Scorchy's mind was on how he'd do the iron work that Mrs. O'Connell wanted done. How was he going to make roses out of metal? He pushed open the door, heard the bell chime...and then heard "Scorchy!" and pulled back just in time to stay the punch his brain was calling up as it spotted the flash of red coming his way.

A young girl had flung her arms around the smith's neck, pulling herself up to land kisses randomly on his face. "Anita?!" he declared while removing her arms from around his neck. "Anita! What are you doing here?!"

Scorchy held Anita at arm's distance as every eye in the joint focused on what was clearly the most exciting thing happening in town at that moment. Ole was nearly overcome with what he felt was his duty to get over to the bar and share what he'd seen, but Wanda had just set down his pie when the girl had nearly knocked the smith over. The boys at the bar would have to wait a bit.

"I came to you! Since you been gone I've missed you. The other boys they aren't like you! Cousin Anna, she says you are a good man, a good man for me. I know you must be lonely. No Ace, no Anna, no shop. You give it all up to keep the trouble away. The trouble it didn't stop..."

"Wanda..." Scorchy said as he turned Anita to face Wanda. Anita stopped in mid-sentence, her smile beaming. "This is Anita. She's the cousin of the wife of my friend Ace. Anita, this is my very good friend Wanda. And this gentleman is Ole."

"We have all met," Anita said. "Your friends are so nice. I will so enjoy this town!" Anita's sparkling brown eyes danced as she looked at Scorchy.

"Anita and I need to take a little walk. Would it be alright to leave her bag here?" Scorchy picked up the old suitcase and stowed it behind the counter before Wanda could respond. As he turned to leave, he looked her fully in the face, "This isn't what it looks like," he said. "It's probably way worse."

Walking around town, stopping occasionally when Anita's gesture-heavy, Latin-based language overcame her, Scorchy made sure that she was clear on several points.

Anita had dreamed up Scorchy's love for her after a bad experience with a gringo outlaw biker. The relationship had not gone down well with family or the club, and when her dad's foot finally came down, her world became the house and close neighbors. The major flaw in her romantic daydream involving Scorchy was that she had no idea where he was. She found the clue she needed written on a scrap of paper stuck on the wall by the phone at her aunt's house. An odd, out of state phone number that directory assistance informed her was in a small town in Montana. Anita had hidden away some money she had earned over the years. Determined to escape her restrictive father, she had set off to find Scorchy and live happily ever after.

Setting Anita straight caused a lot of weeping. Informing her that motorcycle rides and sodas while testing bike repairs did not constitute a commitment to a relationship got Scorchy a slap in the face. Informing her that her father would be called that evening caused her to collapse on a park bench.

Returning to the diner, Scorchy was sure of several things. First and foremost, he had to get Anita home or to Anna. Second, she had to stay someplace that was not with him. Third, it was best not to get the law involved. And fourth...he had no idea how he was going to do any of these things.

Wanda came out from behind the counter, put an arm around Anita, and escorted her to the restroom. Scorchy plopped himself on a counter stool. When he turned around, he noticed the dinner crowd's eyes were squarely on him. Ole was gone and Scorchy imagined he could hear the phone lines singing with rumors that started in Muller's bar the second after Ellen plopped a free cold one in front of him to get him to spill the beans.

As the point man in the migration of the family out of southern California, Scorchy wanted to keep a low profile and yet be on the grid for information that he could then pass on to Ace. Being new and having rolled into town on a chopped Harley Davidson had been enough to get plenty of attention. More he didn't need.

Wanda came out with Anita, who looking much more together. She sat down beside Scorchy while Wanda went off to check on the chattering customers. Necks were turning and eyes glancing at the pair at lunch counter. In loud whispers, men were reprimanded for staring and admonished by their wives to tend to their own business.

"I'm sorry, Scorchy," Anita said. "I don't know what happened to me. Now I don't know what I can do. I make a mess for you here. That Wanda, she is so nice."

Tom walked in and the ambient conversation hushed enough that a whispered "It's the sheriff!" sounded as loud as a cattle auctioneer's call. Tom sat down on the stool next to Scorchy as Wanda slid a coffee cup in front of him. "Thanks, Wanda," He said. Wanda nodded and stepped back, putting the coffee urn back on the hot plate. "Evening, Scorchy."

"Evening, Sheriff."

"Sounds like an exciting day. Am I going to have an exciting evening?"

Scorchy smiled a bit. "One of those kind of afternoons a fella has when he thinks his biggest concern is how to fashion rose flowers for Mrs. O'Connell's fence. Just goes to show how surprising life is."

"There's a plot with a fence Stubby did years ago, way back in the old cemetery," Tom replied. "I can show it to ya. Think ya can figure the pattern." Tom leaned his elbows on the counter, picking up his coffee cup and taking a sip. "You must be Anita. How are you?"

When the diner went quiet Anita had known

it was the cops. Places get quiet when the cops come in. Wanda gave him free coffee, just about everybody gave cops free things. The cops expected it for them coming in. Scorchy didn't seem too worried. She acted like she just belonged there till he called her by name. She expected Scorchy to answer for her, just like home, but he said nothing. Wanda stood back, watching the situation. The other diners, like an audience, hung onto every exchanged word. It was the most exciting thing to happen in town for weeks.

"Yes," Anita finally said. "I am Anita. I am ok. I am sorry that I am causing problems."

"Your folks know where you are?"

"I left a letter that they will have by now." She was looking at her hands now.

"Sherriff, I was hoping to keep outta' the official loop. I know her family and I was going to go call. Her dad will be getting home from work and her mom will be deciding what to tell him, so I figured I'd get the show on the road. He's a man of experience and is respected. He and I can come to an arrangement."

Wanda picked that moment to interject. "I'll be putting her up at my place and she can wash the dishes till Scorchy gets that taken care of." Scorchy hadn't asked, but Wanda could see the situation. There wasn't a hotel in town, no boarding house. The train crews brought living quarters, the "crummies", to sleep in.

183

"Guess I better swing by Muller's and make sure that Ole's got home. Thanks for the coffee, Wanda. Anita was surprised when she saw Tom pull a dime out of his pocket and put it on the counter. "See ya, Scorchy. Let me know."

"Night, Sheriff."

A step away from the counter, Tom turned and glanced at Wanda and Scorchy. He tipped his hat. "Anita, you're a lucky young lady."

Wanda looked out over the customers with a "that's it folks" sort of look. "OK, honey, time to get to work," she said to Anita. "There's an apron by the sink." She watched Anita as she made her way to the back.

She turned back to Scorchy, happy with the look on his face.

"You need a roll of dimes for the phone?"

Bad Wind Comin' to Town

A four door 1959 Chevy Bel Air like the one that pulled into the Chevron the morning the "bad wind" blew into town.

"What's Mom mean when she says she feels a bad wind comin' to town?"

Dad was just sitting down with his coffee and paper at the table. "She said that?"

"Yes, sir, just before she went down the stairs. She looked out the window and said, 'Feels like a bad wind comin.' Does she mean a storm? There isn't a cloud in the sky."

Dad's face took on a serious look for a second, but then he seemed to shake it off as he smiled. "Just something she says now and then." He reached for some freshly stamped and addressed envelopes that were resting on the table near his coffee and handed them to me. "Here, take these letters and drop them in the box at the post office so they get out this morning. You and your sister better get going, don't want to be late for school. See you after. You can help me move the irrigation dams. You can drive the truck!"

Holly and I started out the door, and as the screen door swung closed behind us I heard Dad ask Mom, "Honey, what are you feeling?" Some other kids were coming up the sidewalk and in the midst of greetings and friendly insults Dad's question slipped my mind.

As it turned out, in school was the best possible place I could have been that day, safe and out of the way. I couldn't have had any idea of what mom's "bad wind" was going to bring that day. Now I sometimes fantasize about how I could have maybe just skipped school, been at the shop, backing up Scorchy...but he would have just shooed me off to school. But maybe, just maybe, I could have been in the middle of what became known as "the Stand-Off." Dad never really talked about it. Same with him and his time in the Pacific during the war. I had to get *that* out of other people. The whole untold story of my old man unfolded in, of all places, Germany where I met dad's navigator. He was all too happy to talk when I was buying...but that's another story for another day.

The story of "the Stand-Off" I mostly put together from what old Ole Haralson told me a few weeks later. Since Ole wasn't the center of the action in his own telling of the story and because it only took one beer it's probably pretty close to the truth.

The DJ's of KOOK radio in Billings, Montana. KOOK played a mix of modern pop which made it a popular station with the young and young at heart sets. Major Dan Miller remains a local boardcasting legend at the time of writing.

"And that's the two o'clock news from KOOK in Billings! Back to Major Dan Miller!"

The AM radio on the shelf crackled as it struggled to pull in the signal from Billings. Hank Wills had been working at Mike Swain's Chevron station since he'd come home from Korea. He was pump jockey, janitor, and whatever else Mike needed doing so that he could do oil changes, highway AAA tows, and repairs. Mike had put the station in town after he came home from Europe in World War II and it was the last stop for gas until Laurel.

A Chevron service station attendant cleans a customer's windshield in a period advertisement. In the early 1960's full service was still the norm as was the attendant's uniform appearance.

The *"DING!"* of the customer bell jarred Hank out of his comic book and out the door to the gas pumps. A black, batwing '59 Bel Air sedan sat on the far side of the pump island. The two passengers, men in their twenties, were getting out as Hank approached. Hard muscles under a white t-shirts, their arms were covered with tattoos. "Where's the pisser?" one of them asked.

"Round the side to the right." Hank responded as he bent down to look through the passenger window at the driver. "Fill'er up?"

"Yeah, high test."

The back seat passenger, who went by the name "Beni," pushed the car door closed and bent back down into the open window.

"Tick, you wantin' anything?"

"I want you 'n Slick to hustle it up," the driver

— Tick, it turned out — replied. "I want to get done and gone!"

"Ok, you got it!" Beni said. He was the taller of the two. "Slick, go take a leak, I'm gonna get a Nehi 'n see what's what!!"

A silent, definitive hand gesture came as a response from the shorter and stockier of the pair as he headed around the side of the station to the door marked "Men."

All three men had the same dark shaggy hair, the same degree of beard and moustache, and the same black, plastic-rimmed KD sunglasses covering their eyes. *Kinda like a uniform,* Hank would recall later. It spurred his interest and made him take a closer look.

Hank flipped down the rear license plate, twisted off the cap, and stuck in the nozzle from the high test pump. He set the auto shutoff trigger and went back to the island for the windshield sponge and squeegee. As he was washing the passenger side of the front window, Hank noticed a pistol butt sticking out from under the seat.

"Check under the hood?"

The driver grunted, "Yeah, go ahead."

Hank got the hood up and pulled the dipstick. "You're half a quart down, want it topped off or let it go?"

"Leave it."

"Check the tires?"

"Nah, they're fine. That gas done yet?"

The other two had not come back from the restroom yet and there was an edge to the driver's — Tick's — voice. Hank held down the handle, clicking past the auto shutoff until three dollars worth was all in the tank.

'Three dollars even, mister," Hank called out as he screwed the cap back in place and let the plate slap up...and then, through the rear window, he saw the hack-sawed, raw end of the muzzle of a side-by-side twelve gauge shotgun peeking out from under a blanket on the rear seat. He rounded the car to the driver's side window. "Three dollars even," he repeated.

"Heard you the first time."

NEHI Orange Soda was sold from the vending machine at the local Chevron station.

Hank took three dollar bills from "F.T.W." and "1%" tattooed fingers, rounded back to the front, and closed the hood. Slick finally came round the corner from the restroom with a cigarette hanging from his lips as Beni exited the station front with a nearly empty Nehi orange soda bottle in his hand. He chugged the last of the pop and set the empty on the wiper blade box.

They got into the car and as the driver turned the engine over. Hank thought he heard Beni say, "The old geezer workin' in the garage says the blacksmith shop is just up on Main Street 'n the guy there has a bike. We're in the..." but that's all he could hear as the Chevy pulled away from the pump. It then turned onto the highway, flipped a right, and headed up Main.

Hank went back inside the service station where he reached over the counter and dropped the three dollars into the cash register. "Mike," he said to the older man who was just coming out of the garage. "Those guys had guns in the car. One said something about the blacksmith havin' a bike 'n somethin' else I couldn't make out. The driver has a tattoo on his hand that I saw in a magazine article about motorcycle gangs. You think there is gonna be trouble?"

Mike was already dialing the sheriff before Hank could finish. "I wasn't feeling too good talking to the one guy," He said. "He wanted to know too much about Black and things around town." Mike finished dialing and waited as it rang on the other end. He didn't have to wait long before the sheriff picked up. "Tom? It's Mike at the Chevron.

Got a bad feeling something is happening with the new smith...yeah, Black. Well, we just had some men in here asking about him and Hank says he spotted couple of guns in the..."

"A sawed-off and a pistol!" Hank nearly shouted in excitement. "They said they had the right town 'n turned up Main Street!"

Mike ignored him. "Yeah," he continued over the phone, "I thought you should know. Yeah, I'll call 'em." He hung up.

"Well?" Hank asked.

Mike pulled out the set of Leitz binoculars he'd taken off a Kraut officer near Koblenz during the war. He used them to scan the street up the way the men had gone. "That California car's pullin' in at the smith's shop," he said. "Hank, call Muller down at the bar n' tell him Tom's gonna need some help...and tell him not to come empty handed. Then call Cy Lee and say the same thing. When you're done, follow me."

Hank nodded as he reached for the phone to do as he'd been told. Mike reached under the counter...and pulled out a Winchester M97 trench gun. He laid it on the counter for Hank and reached back under the counter again to produce a lever action 30-30. Then he headed out the door.

A Winchester Model 1897 Trench Shotgun with standard leather military spec sling and top shroud used to protect a soldier's hand from a hot barrel when the weapon was used with attached bayonet. Loaded with 12 gauge buck shot, the '97 proved itself in the trenches of France in 1918, the jungles of the Pacific in World War II, and human wave assaults of Korea. Like many business owners, Mike kept one he brought back behind the counter.

Scorchy Black was in his element. The metal was shaping just the way he saw it in his mind. He rarely had time to do projects for himself, but he'd found the time, and finally he could just see the bear he imagined coming together in the bits of scrap he had collected at his shop. Who says sculptors have to chisel stone?

Scorchy cut the gas and turned off the fan to the forge. As stillness took over the shop, he heard the unmistakable sound of the hammers on a double barrel shotgun being pulled back and a voice he'd hoped to never hear again.

"If it ain't Scorchy Black. Thought you could hide from us? What a naughty boy!"

Turning, he caught just a glimpse of Tick before a fist collided with his head and stars exploded everywhere.

"Get him in the car!"

Scorchy started swinging, connecting with his left. He'd grabbed the hammer from the anvil when Tick slammed the sawed-off butt into his gut...

While all that was going on, Tom's patrol car was screaming down the highway. The gumball was flashing as he raced into town in a cloud of gravel dust. He drove up Main past the smith's shop. Turning the wheel sharply, he flipped a u-turn and pulled up right behind the black Chevy Bel Air, pinning it in against the high curb. Tom got out of the patrol car, keeping his eyes on the door leading into the shop. The door swung open and four men stepped through.

Coming from inside the dim shop, the Big Sky sun dazzled their eyes. Scorchy was in the middle, being strong-armed with a sawed-off shotgun jammed into his back.

"Ok, you fellas," Tom called out. "Hold on right there."

As their eyes adjusted to the blinding stream of sunlight, Tom's dark outline came into focus. His right hand was on the grip of the 1911A1 holstered to his hip. Tom continued...

"Unless Mister Black is going with you of his own volition, I think we have a problem here."

"There's just him," Tick said, not replying to Tom, but thinking out loud more than anything else.

Beni started to move his hand towards the

pistol in his waist band. In the back of his mind a thought flashed...*Why isn't the cop movin'?*

A moment dragged out and the street was quiet except for the sound of chirping bugs and the occasional meadowlark. Then, a low, gravelly voice — not Tom's — came from their left.

"I wouldn't do that."

A glance revealed the pump jockey from the Chevron, his face was hidden behind a pump shotgun tight on the shop corner.

"Back inside," growled Tick

They started to take a step back when the sound of a lever action 30-30 chambering a round into battery came distinctly from behind them, inside the shop.

"Don't turn around and keep where you are!"

It was the voice of the old geezer from that damn gas station! They were cut off and surrounded.

They hadn't expected trouble in a farm town. It was supposed to be peaceful, but Tom had plenty of backup. They hadn't considered nearly all the men in town had served in the military in Asia, Europe, Korea, or someplace else. If they'd thought to look, they might have also noticed that almost every truck in town sported a gun rack. A lot of fellas had military style hardware on those racks. There was no lack of single-action Colt Peacemakers sheathed in leather and handed down from generation to generation, not to mention US or German service side arms, stashed under seats or in jockey boxes.

Muller and Ole had come out of the bar and were now coming up the street to Tom's left side, shotguns raised and ready. Hank was holding his corner of the shop to his right. Tom didn't know for sure, but guessed that the sound of the 30-30 and gravelly voice coming from inside the shop could only belong to Mike. If it came down to shooting there would be a lot of lead coming in. He knew the men backing him up wouldn't back down...and they wouldn't miss.

"You men need to put down the guns and let Mister Black walk out to me," Tom called out. "Then you need to leave our town."

Beni's eyes were bugging out of his head. "Tick," he said, "let's get outta here!"

Tick wasn't having it. "You goin' back ta face Pike and tell him yer yellow?" he said to his underling. "Don't think so. Sheriff, this is a family problem. You don't know nothin' about Black and what he's done. We're like bounty hunters. We're just takin' him back to stand trial...face punishment." Tick had a smirk on his face. "You don't want no biker trash in your town. We're just helpin' you clean up."

"If you're here collecting a bounty, show your warrant from a California judge," Tom said.

"I said we're like..."

"Like nothing...it looks like you're kidnapping a local business owner and citizen in my town."

Tick swung the muzzle of the shotgun from behind Scorchy to press it up under the blacksmith's chin.

"Tom, I'm not worth riskin' any blood over," Scorchy said. "I can take my chances."

"Now ain't that the sensible Scorchy we all know!" Tick said. "Back on off, Tom, before I blow his head off 'n put the next one into you!"

Nobody moved.

In today's world of hostage crisis, law enforcement comes in with SWAT teams, hostage negotiators, command centers, and cops from the county, state, and federal levels...but this was south central Montana in 1965. The law was the local sheriff and his armed citizenry. They were shopkeepers, bartenders, farmers, ranchers...and gas station attendants. Regular guys who all had been part of the military. Volunteers or draftees, their military hitch took them from Montana to serve overseas to defend the country they believed in. That time in uniform took, but also gave back. They might have lost some precious individualism in becoming part of something bigger, risking it all for causes larger than they could comprehend, but getting there with the guy on their left and on their right and their blood and sweat had bought community and safety. Today, it came back as they stood shoulder to shoulder, multi-generations of American soldiers, ready to defend the newest of their own. Those boys were goin' nowhere with the town's new blacksmith. So began "the Stand-off," but time was not going to be a friend to the home team. It was nearly three in the afternoon and soon school would be over and downtown would start to fill up.

Tick pressed the sawed-off harder into Scorchy's chin. "This guy ain't worth yer trouble, he's a double crossing' thief that owes our club. Him and his old buddy ripped us off and nobody rips off our club and gets away with it!"

There wasn't a man not sweating and the tension was ratcheting up. Tom knew his boys could take it. The hand was theirs...a blind man could see it. The wild card was getting' Scorchy out alive and for that something had to happen and fast.

Not far away, a tan International Harvester pick-up sat idling as the driver watched the scene unfold from a distance. The driver summed up the situation in an instant. Easing on the gas, he drove warily from the railroad crossing, round the corner, and up a side street to where it dumped back out on the street. Just before making the corner stop sign at the top of Main Street, he stomped the gas pedal to the floor. Shifting into second gear, he spun the wheel hard right and the empty rear end of the truck fishtailed on gravel. Dust flying the driver hit third and laid on the horn.

The muzzle of the sawed-off jammed into his jaw had Scorchy's senses keyed. He could feel Tick sweating through his own shirt, his body and trigger finger at maximum tension. Over Tick's stressed denouncement of him and Ace, Scorchy heard the sound of a truck suddenly accelerating. Keeping his head as still as possible, his eyes craned up Main where he saw the nose of a truck come into view. Tick took notice, too, as the truck spun around and the horn blared. He shifted slightly, confused by what the truck was doing. Scorchy felt it the instant Tick's tension eased as he was distracted. Lifting his engineer's boot six inches off the ground, he slammed the heavy, thick heel down on Tick's instep while at the same time snapping his head away from the muzzle and throwing his right elbow into Tick's sternum.

Tick's finger muscles spasmed and he pulled the trigger. The 12 gauge roared, blasting the shop sign as Scorchy brought his arm up, sweeping the sawed-off aside and then pushing it back as Tick pulled the second trigger and a hole appeared in the shop's plaster wall.

Beni and Slick, visions of buck shot ripping into their bodies, had their hands up at first blast. Tom reacted at the same time as Tick and Scorchy. He was between them in a flash, spinning and slamming Tick to the wall, then slapping on the cuffs on him almost before he was aware of it. He did a fast frisk, then let him drop to the ground while he was still trying to recover from Scorchy's blow.

Beni and Slick were searched and stood up on the shop wall like prisoners of war with Ole covering them.

The International rolled to a stop and the truck door opened. The driver, seeing everything was well in hand, stepped out and walked over to the group clustered around Tom's car, "Looks like I'm little late."

"Mr. Lee," Scorchy said as he stepped up to my father, "Your timing couldn't have been better! Tick was sweatin' bullets and edging close to blowin' my head off. Tick's a patch holder, answerable to the club prez, Pike. Failing is seriously bad for him. The other two are prospects, sent here to earn their colors. When it got time to jump they figured they liked their lives more than the club." Gazing at the prisoners, he continued, "Yeah, fellas, I know more than I should 'bout all this. I left it behind as clean as I could, but not clean enough. I'm a risk to the town." Scorchy looked at Cy Lee, "I'm a risk to your boy. I'll be packin' up and movin'on."

There was a moment of silence, and then Dad looked at the other men, at Tom, and then back at Scorchy and said, "Like hell!"

Nowadays it would be Miller Time at Muller's Bar. The cops and the SWAT team would have hauled Tick, Beni, and Slick away, never to see light of day. But the only "law" that day was Tom and the citizenry.

I'm not saying who said what because I don't want it coming back on their families. These guys had seen it all, and they wanted their town to stay like it was. Outlaws had come to town and the town had put a stop to their dastardly deeds. They all had known some old hand that had "settled things" in Montana towns in the days of gold, cattle, and railroad rushes.

"What we gonna do with 'em?" someone asked.

"We took care of some SS bastards in the Ardennes," someone else replied. "We could take care of these bums the same way."

"Got no problem with that," said another. "That's how to get rid of problems for good. No wolves in the sheep. We can take 'em up into the Pryors. Nobody gonna find 'em."

The vigilante tone had begun to rise. Beni and Slick's eyes bulged in apprehension. Tick on the other hand had regained his feet and *his* face was one of contempt.

"Send 'em home."

Heads snapped towards Scorchy. The figure-eight of the sawed-off barrel was still red under his chin.

"I've seen what can come of this not ending. Tom, if these three don't get back to the club more will come lookin.' Beni and Slick are club prospects, sent along to earn their club colors, but Ticks a patch-holder. We don't want to be the ones startin' a blood for blood war. Put yer hands down and let's talk," Scorchy said. "Sheriff, take the cuffs off Tick."

Someone said they weren't scared of a bunch of punks and that they'd fight 'em all. I won't say it wasn't Ole. Tom quelled that right off, affirming the courage of the ad-hoc posse but saying town safety came first. "Let's hear what Black has to say." There was no reason for the slightest doubt in Tom's resolve and that was clear even to Tick as the cuffs came off.

"Tick, you tell Pike what happened here. If he wants to settle with me he can come himself and we can meet one-on-one, winner walks away." Scorchy looked to Tom. Tom nodded in affirmation. "Ace n' I have lost all we had. The club's made its point. 'Nuffsenuff.'"

Beni was lookin' eager. Slick was studying the horizon. Tick set his jaw, probably ponderin' the risks both ways. "I'll pass it on to Pike," he finally said. "I won't soon be forgetting this town."

"Reckon, it's time for you three to be getting' outta our town and over the state line before sundown," Tom said. Tom later said he never thought he'd ever get to say that for real in all his time as sheriff.

By 3:15 the three men from California were heading out of town. Their car was thoroughly searched. Guns and ammo were staying in Montana. Tom wasn't budging on that, and he also insisted on escorting them until he could dump them at the Wyoming border and let them go.

Tom made it clear that he had friends at the state and local level all the way into California. He assured Tick that his friends would be happy to work in the spirit of keeping the peace by seeing that they made a timely trip home...OR that an All-Points Bulletin for assault on an officer coupled with flight across state lines could be put out over the radio.

Before he got into his cruiser, Tom thanked the men who'd come to the aide of the town and assured his posse that he was confident that with their show of force the three would head home settling with having made their threats and getting off with no jail time. He was sure when they crossed the Wyoming line they'd be seeing the last of them.

The clock on the bank read 3:20 as Tom's car pulled out on the highway behind the California Chevy. The men looked at each other as their adrenalin started to let down. For most it was the most exciting thing that had happened to them in years.

"Fellas, I'd like to buy all of ya a beer. It's been a hot afternoon," Scorchy said, turning towards Muller. "That is if you feel like puttin' the shotgun down and openin' up."

"I've got the round after that," said my dad.

"And I'll sure drink to that!" Ole cracked, stepping off towards the bar.

I was heading for the shop, just like always, on my way home from school. While the street was kind of empty, there was an odd buzz about. When I got there, the shop door was wide open but Scorchy wasn't inside.

"Hey, Scorchy!"

I pulled my head back through the doorway as the squeak of the sign, pushed by a sudden gust, caught my ear. I was surprised to see that the sign was hanging by only one shackle, the other barely holding on by a bit of wood. The corner was splintered and just a little to the right there was a big hole in the plaster. I stuck my head back through the doorway. "Scorchy! Scorchy, you in here?" I shouted and went inside.

I went back past the counter into the shop. The '53 sat where it always did, but the blanket was off. On the floor was Scorchy's leather jacket. I noticed other things out of place, too. The hammer was on the floor, off the anvil! Blacksmith lore and legend says when the hammers off the anvil the devil can get loose; and from the looks of the shop he'd been there in a rage! I quickly put it back. "Scorchy!" I called out again. "You in here? You ok?"

"Hey, Kid! How was school?"

I felt myself start, getting that zillion volt feeling that a quick shot of adrenaline gives you. I spun around and there was Scorchy. "Wha...what happened to the sign? Man, you scared me! What happened?!"

"A bad wind came through town," Scorchy said. "Made a mess. Coulda' been worse. Way worse." Scorch had a funny grin and I could smell beer.

"Scorch, you doin' ok? Everything ok?"

"Kid, everything is just dandy. Everything is going to be just great! How about you put the blanket back on the bike and help me get the place back to normal."

The Blacksmith shop as it looks today. Notice that the hardware that used to hold up the sign is still there, though the sign itself is long gone.

Glossary

What follows is a list of words and terms selected by a number of early readers of "Me & the '53" for explanation. They are rooted mostly in motorcycle and military culture or American 20th Century history. The Glossary is laid out from the beginning to the end of the book so you can either pre-read or thumb through as you go through the chapters.

* * *

California Biker Wars: A conflict between various "1%" and "outlaw" motorcycle clubs over control of areas of California. The rivalry continues today, often fueled by illegal activities such as control of drug trafficking.

Flat Track Course: An oval race track course without banked sides around which riders raced their motorcycles a predetermined number of laps. Flat tracks could be set up anywhere there was space and provided the outlaw racing clubs areas to compete outside the large organized races set up by the AMA.

American Motorcycle Association (AMA): Organized in the mid-1920s to support the motorcycle industry and riders. It became the overall organization of American riders and remains so today. In the post-World War II American motorcycle culture various groups broke away from the AMA's event sanctioning setting up what became known as outlaw clubs and events.

Panhead: A style of Harley-Davidson motorcycle engine so named because of the distinct shape of the valve rocker covers. The engine is a two-cylinder pushrod V-twin design. The "panhead" replaced the "knucklehead" starting in 1948 and was manufactured until 1965 when it was replaced by the "shovelhead." As the design of Harley-Davidson engines evolved through the years, the distinctive shape of the valve covers has allowed Harley enthusiasts to classify an engine simply by looking at the shape of the covers. The panhead design resembles an upside-down pan.

Ivy League: A group of 8 private colleges in the northeastern United States. Founded before or just after the establishment of the United States, the colleges have long been thought of as the pinnacle of the American education system. Graduates from these schools are often thought of as rich and privileged.

Dick Dale, legendary early rock guitarist, on his "chopped" 1941 Harley.

Chopped: Term for motorcycle that has had stock parts, normally fenders, removed or cut down. The removal of "excess" parts was at first a means to reduce weight and later came to reflect rider style and trends.

Seabees: A Seabee is a member of the United States Navy Construction Battalion or CB from which the name Seabee is derived. The Seabees have a history of building military bases, bulldozing and paving thousands of miles of roadways and airstrips, and a myriad of other construction projects, often under enemy fire, dating back to World War II.

Hells Angels: The best known of the outlaw clubs started after World War II with the name suggested by Arvid Olsen, an associate of the founders, who had served in the Flying Tigers' "Hell's Angels" squadron in China during World War II. The club became well known under the leadership of the Oakland chapter, at the time headed by Sonny Barger. That chapter's winged skull colors are taken from an 8th Air Force bomber that flew out of England during World War II. The club is still one of the most predominate in the outlaw motorcycle world and continues to be the best known, it logo and name being trademarked. Note that there is no apostrophe in "Hells."

Moniker: An informal term for a name.

Galvanized: A zinc protective covering electrically plated onto iron or steel.

Chuck Taylors: A popular shoe designed in 1917 by the Converse Company. The high topped athletic shoe had a canvas top with rubber bottom and was promoted in the 1920s as a basketball shoe designed by basketball great "Chuck" Taylor and the Converse All-Stars in schools and at public events. By the 1960s they were the most popular shoe in US sports and were worn as street shoes by many kids. They remain a popular shoe in many areas of Americana culture.

The Depression: Also "The Great Depression," was a severe worldwide economic depression during the decade preceding World War II. The timing of the Great Depression varied across nations, but in most countries it started in 1930 and lasted until the late 1930s or middle 1940s. It was the longest, deepest, and most widespread economic downturn of the 20th century. People of all walks of life were devastated by the loss of jobs and income.

Nationalist China and Communist China: Following the revolutionary overthrow of the Nationalist — the first non-Imperial Chinese government — in 1948 by the Communist lead forces of Mao Zedong, China was divided into two parts with two separate governments. With the communists ruling the mainland, the Nationalist government went into exile on the island of Taiwan. The government in Taiwan was recognized by the UN and the US as the official government of China until the diplomatic missions of President Nixon thawed relationships with the mainland, communist government which in turn brought recognition by the US and the UN. The nationalist party still maintains political control over Taiwan and they are recognized and are a treaty protected ally of the US. To this day the communist government claims Taiwan as part of China.

VJ-Day: Victory Over Japan Day was declared on September 2, 1945 with the official signing of the Japanese surrender document on the deck of the battleship USS Missouri in Tokyo Bay ending World War II.

American Volunteer Group (AVG): The "Flying Tigers" was a group of American military and civilians who were hired in a covert mission to help the Nationalist Chinese Air Force fight the invading Japanese. Led by Claire Chennault, a retired US Army Air Corps officer and pilot, the American volunteers went to China and flew

Curtis P40 Warhawk aircraft alongside Chinese and Royal Air Force pilots before the Japanese attacked Pearl Harbor.

Aurora: A company that made very popular, simple glue together plastic model kits available in the 1960s.

Jap Zero: The Mitsubishi A6M was a long range single engine fighter plane used during World War II. Named the "Zero" by allied forces for identification., the aircraft was widely encountered and could take on any American aircraft at the time.

Wrench: A slang term for a mechanic.

Flux: A chemical cleaning agent that promotes the clean adhesion of welds during soldering.

Moonshiner or Bootlegger: Someone who produces and distributes distilled alcohol — often know as "moonshine" or "white lightening" — illegally. "Bootlegger" refers to those who moved the product to market, and many became legendary for their fast cars which would outrun law enforcement. These mechanically improve "hot rods" became the basis for the now popular sport of stock car racing.

Radial Fighter Aircraft Engine: A radial aircraft

engine is designed with the cylinders in a circle as opposed to being inline. Radial engines allowed all the cylinders to have cooling air push past them in equal amount and therefore did not require any radiator for liquid cooling. Many pilots believed the radial design to be a tougher and safer engine as it did not require liquid cooling.

Civy Clothing: Normal clothing worn by soldiers when they are not in uniform or issue clothing. Looking like a civilian.

Hobo Jungle: A campsite established in or near railway yards where men and women who traveled by "hopping" freight trains to get to their destinations lived. The "jungle" provided a place where these hobos or bums, as they were known, could find food and shelter without going into the town or city which often meant arrest and jail.

Tinker Toy: A wooden toy that uses various length rods designed to fit in to specifically shaped joint blocks to make structures limited only by imagination.

IGA: The Independent Grocers Alliance is an organization of independent store aligned for purposes of buying grocery and other goods. Often these stores are the only grocer in a small community that is not large enough to support a major grocery chain.

Tony and Riff, West Side Story: A modern musical retelling of the Romeo and Juliet story set in New York City's West Side. Pitting two rival gangs — the Sharks and the Jets — against each other, Tony is the Romeo character to Maria's Juliet, and Riff is Tony's life-long friend and leader of the Jets. In an early scene in the movie, Riff visits Tony at his job and they go into the alley where they pull bottles of soda from wooden crates and remove the bottle top by slapping them against the edge of a metal trash can, a fad every boy who saw the movie had to master.

Korean War: A conflict that developed after World War II to keep the southern part of the Korean peninsula in the political orbit of the west and the United States. The communist north invade the south, drawing the United Nations into a protracted, yet undeclared, war. It was the first of many "proxy" wars fought for dominance of the world political spheres. The Soviet Union and the Communist Chinese sought expand their influence by supporting the military of the north while the UN — mainly the US — supported the South. The fighting lasted from 1950 to 1954 when a ceasefire was signed, however, the area remains a political and military hot bed to this day.

Vietnam War: Much like the Korean War, the US became involved as the Communist Peoples Republic of Vietnam tried to militarily take over the southern Republic of Vietnam. Major US engagement began in the mid-1960s, escalating into major combat before ending in 1975. After withdrawal of US forces, the Army of the Republic of Vietnam was not able to withstand the forces of the north which were receiving logistical and arms support from the Soviet Union. Vietnam is now one country and has sought, more and more, to be a part of the western sphere of trade.

63C, Military Occupational Specialty (MOS): Describes what a soldier is trained to do as part of the army. In Scorchy's case, he was a vehicle mechanic, a 63C or "Charlie." Elvis was a 19D (Cavalry Scout). The author joined the US Army as an 11B (Combat Infantry Soldier).

Tread-head: Army slang term for a tank crewmember.

Kaserne: German word for military post or base. After World War II the US Army took over many of the German bases permanently and chose to call them "kasernes" instead of "barracks," "camps," or "forts."

Gelnhausen: A small town in the central German state of Hessen. Located east of Frankfurt, Gelnhausen was the location of Coleman Kaserne and the 3rd Brigade of the 3rd Armored Division.

Motor Pool: Area of a military post that contains

the maintenance and parking for military vehicles.

M59 Armored Personnel Carrier (APC): A fully armored tracked vehicle designed to carry infantry soldiers into battle alongside tanks. The vehicle resembled a pointed shoe box on tank tracks with a large door in the back.

M37: A Dodge three-quarter ton, 4 wheel drive general purpose truck used from the early 1950s until the Vietnam conflict.

Stars & Stripes Newspaper & Book Store: The Stars & Stripes Newspaper has served the US military forces as a source of independent news printed in their locations since 1861. The European Stars & Stripes prints a daily edition that covers US, world and local military news and is available to soldiers at a number of outlets. Stars & Stripes also operates book stores on US military bases, providing soldiers and their family members with access to American magazines and books. The book store was always busy when new magazines that catered to individual interests arrived. Most of the Stars & Stripes bookstore managers knew their customer base and were always ready to put them in touch with America back home.

NCO: "Non Commissioned Officer" or sergeants in the enlisted chain of command who make sure all the jobs needed for the Army to function are carried out in good military order.

3rd Armored Division: Formed during World War II and fighting in Europe against Nazi Germany, the division returned to German in 1956. Its brigades were originally located east of Frankfurt to defend against possible Soviet invasion.

Wildflecken, Grafenwoher or Graf, and Hohenfels: Three major training areas where soldiers of the 3rd Armored Division trained in combat-like conditions. Wildflecken is located near the border between the Federal Republic of Germany and the German Democratic Republic (pre-reunification) near the Fulda Gap. Located in a mountainous area, the training area is often in clouds.

Bundeßtrasse B-40: A two-lane highway (not autobahn) running from Frankfurt to Fulda. The road traveled by military convoys during training and deployment to the border to face the Soviet military during the cold war.

Fulda: A major German city on the border of the Federal Republic and situated in the Fulda Gap (the traditional path of invasion from the east into western central Germany and Europe).

West and East Germany: From 1945 until 1990, Germany was divided into two countries: the Federal Republic of German (West Germany, which was aligned with the US and Western Europe) and the German Democratic Republic (East Germany, which was aligned with the Soviet Union). A fortified border ran between the two countries (the "Iron Curtain"). With the economic collapse of the Soviet Union, the two Germany's reunited in 1990.

Under the eye of East German and Soviet soldiers workers put the first cement blocks in place dividing Berlin. This wall would eventually extend from the Baltic Sea in the north to the Bavarian Border in the south.

Iron Curtain: The division between the free western European nations and the communist controlled areas of Eastern Europe. The term was coined by Winston Churchill during a speech in which he stated that "an iron curtain has fallen across Eastern Europe" as the Red Army refused to allow the any but favorable communist governments to take power. With the demise of the Soviet Union in the 1990s, the Iron Curtain was drawn.

White Light: A term used in the military for using normal vehicle headlights in the dark.

Black Out Drive: A system that allows military vehicles to be driven in the darkness without giving away their location to the enemy. Small, low powered lights provide markers on each vehicle. Drivers must adjust their vision to darkness so they can see, often wearing read goggles to prepare.

Bivouac Area: Place where soldiers set up their tents when they are not in the barracks.

American Forces Network (AFN): A radio and television system set up where American Forces are stationed bring familiar programming to GIs.

Bent Neck Flashlight (with red filter): The standard issue military flash light is made of olive green plastic and had 90 degree bend at the top so it can be stood on end to provide light. Each flashlight has a set of colored filter lenses stored in screw on cap the bottom, the red lens is used for all night illumination and is usually always covering the bulb.

GI: Slang term for an American Army soldier coined during World War II from "Government Issue" that was often teamed with another slang term for a soldier, "Joe." "GI" was used to describe, usually derogatively, items provided the soldier from food to toilet paper.

Flak: A term for strong criticism about something you have done or are trying to do. It comes from the German abbreviation for "Flugzeugabwehrkanone" or antiaircraft artillery. When bomber crews flew over Germany in World War II, they would talk about how bad the enemy fire, as in "The Flak was so thick you could walk on it."

Breaker Bar: A long metal pry bar used to separate sections of armored vehicle track. A handy item for prying and lifting as well.

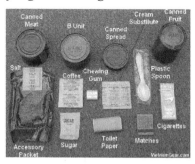

C-Rations: Military meals developed during World War II that provided a soldier a complete precooked meal in small cans inside a small cardboard box. The meals could be eaten warmed or cold out of the can.

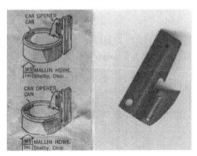

Each soldier carried a small can opener (the P38 can opener, above) on his dog tag (ID tag) chain so he did not have to wait for others to open and eat his meal.

Specialist 5th Class: A military rank used for soldiers who have the time in service and grade to be a Sergeant, but who are in a technical position snd not leading troops. This came from the Technical Sergeant rank of World War II. Scorchy, as a 63C, has experience, skill and ability in his job but is not generally required to direct the work of other soldiers. To make sure he has the pay and privileges of an NCO, he has been promoted to the grade Specialist 5th Class.

Mess Hall Joe: Coffee made in the mess hall, the large industrial pots never stopped brewing and often just new water and coffee grounds were added on top of old coffee to keep the troops on night duty awake till morning.

Air/Army Post Office (APO): Moves mail from the US to Army and Air Force bases world-wide so that postage is kept at the same rate as stateside. For those overseas they can send mail without charge inside the APO system. Each Kaserne has an APO number (like a ZIP code). Scorchy's at Coleman Kaserne was 39. When the US Postal Service initiated the five digit ZIP Code, the military revised its APO system and Coleman Kaserne changed from APO 39 to APO 09091.

Barry Sadler, "Ballad of the Green Berets": A US Army Special Forces Combat Medic and Staff Sergeant wounded in Vietnam, Sadler wrote a song about the US Special Forces, the "Ballad of the Green Berets." The song was Number One on the Billboard Top 100 for five weeks. Wearing his Army dress uniform and Green Beret, Sadler performed on various TV shows such as The Ed Sullivan Show.

Pony Express: A short lived cross country mail carrier that used skilled riders on fast horses that ran between stations located about every 10 miles. At each station the rider would leap off his horse with the mail pouches and do a running mount, leaping onto the back of the next horse held ready for him. The service was replace by the telegraph and train but became symbol of the rugged west and those who won it and was often seen in movie and TV westerns.

Ed Sullivan Show: A popular TV variety show on the CBS network that ran every Sunday from 1948 to 1971. Hosted by New York entertainment columnist Ed Sullivan, the show often was the first stop to stardom for musical acts such as the Beatles, Rolling Stones and many others.

Jackhammer Grips: An early style of rubber hand grips used on custom motorcycles.

Shindig: A term for party, event, or celebration.

Tōjō-Hideki: A general of the Imperial Japanese Army, the leader of the Imperial Rule Assistance Association, and the 40th Prime Minister of Japan during most of World War II, from October 17, 1941 to July 22, 1944. Tōjō was the Hitler of Japan, and was held accountable for the war on the United States.

POW: Prisoner of War.

Payment Kitty: A term that refers to a group payment to a specific end. Often a jar or vase is used to collect the money,

A Rambler station wagon like the one Errol drove.

Rambler Wagon: A type of automobile called a "station wagon," it was the forerunner of the mini-van and was produced by the Nash Rambler Company. Noted not for looks but for durability, the Rambler was the auto of many families in the 1950s and 60s.

Racing Pillion Pad: A small rectangular wedge shaped leather covered pad that was attached to the rear fender of flat track racing motorcycles to allow the driver to sit further back on the bike to get into a more aerodynamic crouch over the gas tank of the bike. Since most bikers raced the motorcycle they rode on a daily basis, the pad became commonplace and provided a small amount of passenger comfort. The pad could be replaced with a stock or custom luggage rack.

Tang: An orange flavored fruit drink powder mix that was brought on the market by General Foods in 1959, however, it did not become a national trend until astronaut John Glenn drank it as part of food experiments on the first orbital space mission in 1962.

Cousin Eddie (played by Randy Quaid), wearing a dickey in National Lampoon's Christmas Vacation.

Dickey: Part of the fashion trend of the 60s was wearing a turtle neck sweater under a shirt or sweater. A dickey was a false turtleneck with just enough cloth attached to provide the correct look of a total sweater.

British Invasion: Led by what became probably the most popular rock band in history, the Beatles, America was introduced to Anglicized version of mostly covers of American influenced rock music. Presented as a total package of personality, fashion and music by American record companies, the trend caught hold with a string of bands appearing on TV variety shows such as Ed Sullivan and the Smothers Brothers causing female fan screaming meltdown The Beatles were followed by other bands such as The Rolling Stones, Herman and the Hermits, Gerry & the Pacemakers, The Small Faces, The Spencer Davis Group, The Zombies, and The Who.

Go-Go Boots: A short flat heeled half calf length boot worn during the 1960s to the present day. The term go-go comes from a French expression meaning abundance of joy and happiness and the slang term "go" which meant something that was in fashion or the rage with the group. Women wearing these boots as well as other "Mod" attire soon became the club and TV rage as they danced on elevated platforms and were known as "Go-Go Girls."

Mod Look: "Mod" or "Modernist" culture rose up in Britain in the 1950s based on jazz, blues, and other forms of "new" music and included a strict fashion code for both men and women based on the newest and most fashionable items. The British Invasion, especially the Beatles, brought this fashion trend with its tight pants, jackets, and shoes. Girls wore the required short "mini" skirt, go-go boots, and fishnet stockings. Mod culture in Britain was captured in the Who rock opera *Quadraphina* which was made into film.

All Ahead Full: A nautical term for maximum speed for a ship, and a navy term for getting after something as fast as you can.

Where the Action Is: A Dick Clark produced TV variety show that ran from 1965 to 1967 headlined by the US rock band Paul Revere and the Raiders. It introduced new musical talent to a youth audience. A daily afternoon program that was followed by "Dark Shadows," which was a teen oriented vampire soap.

Paul Revere & the Raiders: An American rock band that brought out number of hits in the mid to late 1960s and early 70s such as "Kicks" which was ranked by Rolling Stone as one of the 500 greatest songs of all time. The group wore American Revolutionary war uniforms and played off of Revere's name as a counter to the British Invasion

Trip Hammer: A large device that uses a motor to lift a heavy weighted hammer into a raised, locked position that is then release by pushing with the foot on a bar. The motor raises and drops the hammer as long as the smith's foot is on the release bar, allowing him to move the metal being shaped under the constant stream of blows.

Forge, Forge Fan: The forge is used to heat up metal to high temperatures so it can be worked. Most modern forges burn propane or natural gas and are brought to a high temperature with a fan that forces oxygen into the flame. Originally, the forge was fired by wood or coal and the smith would fan the flames with a bellows that was made of folded leather and wood which sucked in a large amount of air and then compressed and forced it through a small opening into the forge to increase the heat.

Gringo: A Mexican term for white Americans.

Crummies: Rail road cars that were converted into living quarters for rail gangs that repaired the nation's rail roads. A reference to the condition of living in them.

KD Sunglasses: Ray-Ban sunglass with black plastic frames introduced in 1952. Worn by movie idol James Dean, they became popular with motorcycle riders.

Sawed-Off 12 Gauge Shotgun: A standard double barreled, normally side by side model, that has had the barrels sawn down to length less of 12 inches or less and the wooden stock cut off leaving only a hand grip for the purpose of concealment. It is an illegal weapon in most situations that is used for intimidation at closer range. The 12 gauge refers to the size of the cartridge, 12 gauge being the largest and most popular hunting type.

Dip Stick: Refers to a measuring gauge that checks the oil in an automobile engine. It is a metal stick that follows a tube to the bottom of the engine where the oil pan is located. The end is marked to indicate when more oil needs to be added for safe operation of the vehicle. The use requires no real skill, simply remove it, clean off the oil with a rag, insert it back in the tube, and then remove it again. If the oil sticks at a level below the manufacture's specification the required amount is added. Service station attendants would try to up-sell oil along with a fill up of gasoline.

FTW and 1%er: "FTW" stands for "Fuck the World" and 1%er indicates belonging to what the AMA called the 1% of the American motorcycle riding populace who were members of outlaw clubs.

Kraut: A derogatory GI slang term during World War II for Germans based on the German pickled cabbage dish *sauerkraut* or *kraut*.

Koblenz: A city in the western part of Germany situation at the confluence of the Rhine and Mosel Rivers, known for wine production.

Leitz Binoculars: A brand name of a German optical lens manufacturer who produced binoculars in Wetzlar, Germany. American GIs perceived German optics as superior to their own national brands and these were prime war booty brought back for hunting.

M97 Trench Gun: A militarized version of the

Winchester pump action shotgun. The shotgun was shortened and modified with a heat shield over the barrel and a bayonet mounting lug and was used for close range combat in the trenches of World War I. The M97 was limited to security and military police roles in World War II and was sold at surplus after the war. Its size, price, and 12 gauge fire power made it popular for business defense.

1911A1 Pistol: A US military pistol designed by John Browning to provide US service member with a semi-automatic (the pistol's action brings a new cartridge into battery each time the trigger is pulled until the magazine is empty). The pistol holds 8 .45 caliber cartridges specially designed for the pistol. Used from before the First World War the pistol was used by the military until the 1990s. After World War II many found their ways home with returning veterans who knew and valued their robust character and firepower.

Brought Into Battery: When a cartridge is stripped from the magazine or clip that holds it and then pushed into the firing chamber, ready to be struck by the firing pin, it is said to "be in battery." In the story this is done by actuating the lever of the Winchester 30-30 rifle.

Single-Action Colt Peacemaker: The Colt Firearms Company under the leadership of Samuel Colt developed a six shot, single action (the hammer has to be pulled back each time the pistol is fired), revolving cylinder pistol. While made in many calibers, the most common was the .45 caliber. The simplified loading process, using brass cased cartridges, made the pistol simple to load and use. The "Peacemaker" comes from its wide use by law officers in the west and because it was within the price range of many settlers, allowing them to protect their families, farms, and ranches from desperados and Indian war parties.

Military Draft: In the US, the Selective Service which in the time of declared war requires the military service of all able-bodied male citizens. The US maintains the requirement that 18-year-old males register with the Selective Service, however, there has been no call-up or draft since the end of the Vietnam War. During the time of the draft, soldiers who did not volunteer were typically assigned to combat units and given no choice of military occupational specialty (MOS). Scorchy voluntarily enlisted, and so was able to choose his MOS to training and education he feels will be helpful to him in the future.

Rip-off: Slang for to steal or take from someone or organization, often by over charging for a service. The gang members accuse Scorchy and Ace of either taking club parts from the shop or overcharging for services performed on club bikes. The term is also used when something such as a song or idea is taken and used by someone without the permission of the owner (i.e. "They ripped of my song lyrics!").

Engineer Boots: Boots originally designed by the Chippewa boot company during the depression to provide tough work boot without laces. The boot featured a round toe, mid-calf or taller upper made of tough leather, the lowers often with reinforced or steel toes, and hard rubber sole. Straps at the ankle and the top secured the boot to the foot and leg. Often waterproofed, they became the footwear of choice for the American motorcycle rider.

SS Bastards in the Ardennes: Waffen-SS soldiers who were the spearhead troops of the German military. They were a politically motivated arm of the Wehrmacht, whose origin stemmed from the original body guard for Hitler. They were blamed for several incidences of executions of American prisoners of war such as the Malmedy Massacre during the Battle of the Bulge which was fought in late 1944 and early 1945 in the area of the Ardennes Forest. When word spread of the massacre, Germans identified with the Waffen-SS were no long taken alive.

Pryors: The Pryor Mountains that make up the western edge of the Crow Indian Reservation.

Reader & Book Club Questions

- What was unique about the setting of "Me & the '53" and how did it enhance or take away from the story?

- What specific themes did the author emphasize throughout the novel? What do you think he or she is trying to get across to the reader?

- Do the characters seem real and believable? Can you relate to their predicaments? To what extent do they remind you of yourself or someone you know?

- How do characters change or evolve throughout the course of the story? What events trigger such changes?

- In what ways do the events in "Me & the '53" reveal evidence of the author's world view?

- Did certain parts of the book make you uncomfortable? If so, why did you feel that way? Did this lead to a new understanding or awareness of some aspect of your life you might not have thought about before?

- Did the photos help you to understand some of what the Kid, Scorchy, Wanda or Ace had experienced or seen in their lives or this time period?

- There are people you may know who are Kid's age, perhaps relatives or family friends. Has this book helped you understand their life or perhaps provide you with some questions to talk about with them?

- Do you think that today it would be possible for someone of Kid's age to have the same kind of experiences? What could still be the same? Are some things impossible to imagine now?

Acknowledgements

First up is my daughter, Anna. Thanks for the sharing love of writing and always being positive about my stories! It was writing stories to share at the writers' group with you that brought this story concept out in the first place.

The Libby Writer's Group and especially Megan. Thanks for inviting Anna to the group. That forced my hand and I had to get a story into a chapter to share. The group's acceptance of the first chapter got me rolling on the rest of the book.

Without the tech help and the old school biker look at the chapters by Kevin and Billy detail would have suffered. Plus the acceptance and encouragement for more story from these cats made me believe I had something to share.

Syd, thanks for the first edit and helping me find some of those voices!

Scott, thanks for the page layout, cover, edit and support through this. I don't want to think where I would be at without your help now! Thanks!

A Bit about Cyrus Lee

Cyrus's early years were spent moving from one US Navy base to another during his father's tour of duty. With his dad's retirement the family moved to the south central Montana town where "Me & the '53" takes place. After a few more years the family moved to up the highway to Billings where Cyrus spent his teen and early adult life.

Following graduation from Billings West High, then Eastern Montana College, with a few classes at the school of hard knocks. In 1979 Lee enlisted in the US Army and was stationed in Germany. Lee returned to the US in 1994 after time a soldier and Department of Defense Dependent Schools teacher settling with his wife Kim and small children in Libby, Montana.

Starting over in Montana, his first job was as a wild land firefighter. Independent photojournalism, the Montana Army National Guard, and an educational administrative position at the new Head Start program in Libby kept Lee busy until he took his online business, Soldat FHQ, to a full time status. Expanding interest and family pushed him to open a storefront which combined

Soldat FHQ with Flying Tiger Hobby Shop. Soldat has provided costuming, props and set design to movie and theater productions.

Lee first wrote "Me & the '53" in 2013 as an e-book and has since independently published several revisions of it in print. Lee lives with his wife Kim in Libby, Montana.

A Bit about Kevin Poole

Kevin was born at Burtonwood Royal Air Force Station, in Burtonwood, England during his dad's overseas tour with the US Air  Force. Spending his early years in Arkansas, he moved to Billings when his father, a "Wildcat" geologist, relocated to Montana to hunt for oil.

Poole graduated from Billings West High School, same class as Lee, in 1972. It was Poole who introduced Lee to Harley Davidsons and they have built and ridden Harley Davidsons since their teen age years in the 1970s.

Kevin Poole is now a well-known and respected retro custom bike designer and builder as well as a painter with part of his classic education coming from a number of bikers who left California in the 60s relocating to Montana. Combing old regional farms, ranches and businesses for over the past near half century he has acquired what is one of the largest vintage part collection and inventory in the area. Poole is a credited scenic movie and commercial artist. He has been a Harley shop mechanic and a carney.

More of "Me & the '53"

Future Companion novels to "Me & the '53" are in the planning stages. They will connect the reader to the characters with the highlights, the life, adventures and travels of Ace, Scorchy, and Wanda.

I always want to hear reader's comments and ideas. "Me & the '53" has a Facebook Page at www.facebook.com/MeThe53/.

I wrote this with the young adult reader in mind and I would appreciate you sharing the book with your school and public librarians for inclusion in their stacks. I am available for readings and youth writing seminars.

Think this would be a great movie? So do I, if that is your thing let's talk!

Ace Murphy's Motorcycle merchandise is available on Facebook as well (just search for Ace Murphy's).

Other Works

Poole and Lee worked together on "My Daddy Rides a Harley" in 1977. Never widely distributed, the somewhat autobiographical fully illustrated book, it shows a bit of the period local biker culture.

Made in the USA
Columbia, SC
25 June 2018